THE
CARD

JIM DEVITT

This is a work of fiction. The characters, places and events in this book either are a product of the author's imagination or are used fictitiously. Certain real locations and public figures are incidental to the plot, and are not intended to change the entirely fictional character of the work.

To Melissa,
you inspired me to follow my dream.

ACKNOWLEDGMENTS

I'd like to thank the following people, without their support I would still be staring at Chapter One.

Melissa, without you there would be no book. Thank you for your brainstorming, editing, chopping and artwork. Thank you for your encouragement and support, and most of all, believing in our dreams.

A special thanks to my Mother-In-Law, Ada Ruiz Garcia and my parents, John and Muriel, who didn't laugh out loud when I asked them to read and edit a novel that I wrote.

Thank you to Marsha Rollinger for putting up with me throughout the graphic design process and for creating a great cover.

Finally, I want to thank the others who selflessly donated their time and energy to move this dream forward, Gemma Morales, Scott Callahan and Tony Valente.

THE CARD

CHAPTER
1

Silence dominated our drive until Dad broke the ice, "I've got something for you."

"Something for me?" I asked.

The steel framework of the retractable roof soared across the sky as we approached the looming stadium. With every block, my heart pounded harder against the walls of my chest. A nauseous feeling rumbled in my stomach.

"I hope it's some Pepto-Bismol. I can't believe how nervous I am."

"C'mon, Van, you'll be fine. I'm really proud of you."

"I don't even know what I'm doing. I had one afternoon of training that consisted of, '… here's your locker, here's where the bats go, don't talk to anyone and never ask for autographs.'"

"Just relax and have fun. You went through a lot to get this gig. You beat out hundreds of kids to get this chance. You're the first one in the family to make it to the big leagues. Go ahead, check the glove box," Dad said as he pointed across the dashboard.

With a click, I whipped open the small door and inside sat a wrapped box. "What is it?"

"Just open it already."

The traffic slowed outside the stadium. Through the open window, I felt the energy of opening day. After ripping open the box, I withdrew a lone baseball card. My puzzled look told the story. "Thanks, Dad. Who's Moe Berg?"

"A relatively unknown player that bounced around a little bit back in the 1920's and 1930's. I've always been fascinated by him. Who knows, maybe the card is worth something."

Sitting at a red light, I examined the card and looked up to catch Dad staring ahead with a distant look.

He snapped out of his daze and said, "You should always hang on to this card—it's special."

"Of course—I will," I said as we pulled up to Safeco Field.

"Mom and I will be back later for the game. Look for us, if you can. We can't wait to see you in action."

I placed the card in my backpack and stepped into the sunshine. I took a deep breath and looked up at the façade. The glass and brick entrance yielded to the giant steel framework of the retractable roof, which squatted like a giant beetle over the rail yard. With no chance of rain, the rounded structure sat in an open position. I jumped at the blast of a train horn and started toward the gate. A few fans milled about with opening day optimism, looking at me with an expression of "Who's that?", as I approached the player's entrance.

Feeling uncomfortable with the attention, I hurried to the gate.

"Hi'ya, Van. Are you ready for the big day?" Charlie asked. He opened the gate with his weathered hands and gave me a big smile, partially hidden by his white, bushy mustache. He acted as if he had known me for years, even though I only met him yesterday.

"Uh, sure, I guess," I said.

"Ah, don't worry. You'll be fine. I've seen tons of kids come through here in the last fifteen years, and you're the best of any of them. I can tell. I have a special knack for figuring people out. That's what has kept me alive for so long."

"What do you mean?"

"Oh, trust me. I met many a bad guy working as a Seattle Police officer for thirty years."

"Wow, that must've been cool. I guess things are a lot quieter around here, aren't they?"

"Oh, you bet they are. I'd probably do this for free, but don't tell anyone," he said with a chuckle.

"I've got to get inside. See you later," I said, moving into the darker reaches of the stadium. Around me, people buzzed with activity, the kind that can only be associated with opening day. Workers stacked cases of giveaways by the entrance gates, a Cushman whizzed by with bags of ice dripping off the back and I walked through a crowd of new wide-eyed interns listening to instructions from their boss.

With the excitement building, I picked up my pace. The pale yellow walls of the tunnel behind-the-scenes contrasted with the beauty that existed beyond the catacombs. I followed the natural curve of the hallway as the exposed pipes snaked along overhead.

Arriving at the visiting clubhouse, I pulled open the door. My nervous excitement grew as I walked down the long clubhouse to the far corner. The room was raucous as the players dressed for the game, with laughter and music filling the space. An Oakland Athletics uniform hung in my locker.

Sitting down, I pulled out my iPhone and logged into the web browser. After typing in *Moe Berg*, I read the entries. Clicking on *Beckett Baseball Card Price Guide*, I entered *Berg*. There weren't many listed and mine wasn't a rookie card, so it was worthless.

"No phones in here. I don't want to catch you on your phone ever again or you're out of here," Greg Napolini shouted. The visiting clubhouse manager ruled over this domain since the beginning of baseball in Seattle.

"Sorry, I didn't know," I said while throwing my phone and the card into the locker.

Changing into my uniform, I pushed and felt the fabric stretch as my redheaded mop popped through. I guess my almost six-foot frame was a little bigger than most batboys. I laced up my cleats, grabbed my glove and jogged down a corridor leading to the dugout.

Trotting up the steps to field level, I caught a cleat on the last one. Stumbling, I quickly turned it into a walk, hoping that nobody noticed. The stands were almost full and a buzz of crowd noise filled my ears. The open roof squatted over the right field bleachers, casting an ominous shade. The rest of the stadium basked in brilliant sunshine, perfect for opening day.

I felt as if I had just won the lottery, all of this because I was lucky enough to have won an essay contest. During the many interviews, I never dreamed that I would actually get to be on the field. Walking toward the end of the dugout, I allowed myself a little smile.

The shouts echoed from the crowd.

"Peanuts, programs."

"Ice cold beer."

"Freeze your teeth, give your tongue a sleigh ride—ice cold bea hea."

Around me, I watched the high fives, fist bumps and laughing from a hundred different people that included players, trainers, coaches, photographers and other media types.

Interrupting my excitement, a man with a clipboard and headset walked toward me with his arms outstretched, as if he was trying to herd a flock of chickens. "Let's get you in the right place for the introdu—" he stopped mid sentence. "Oh, you're the batboy. Wow, you sure are bigger than most. I thought you were one of the players."

He continued into the crowd, lining up the Oakland players. On cue, he sent them to the third base line, synchronized with the public address system introductions.

The first few chords of the National Anthem brought a lump to my throat. I stood near the dugout holding my cap over my heart. As the music reached its crescendo, the crowd grew louder and my eyes welled up with emotion. The cheering fans muffled the final notes, then the fireworks erupted, the smoke dissipated and the sulfur smell of spent gunpowder drifted down on the most beautiful setting I had ever seen.

The view from the field was a different one than from the stands. The crowd, perfectly positioned, faced directly at the infield. I realized that the 47,166 fans did not even know that I existed. However, it felt like I had all 94,332 eyeballs focused on me. A constant and growing murmur filled the stadium as the players came into the dugout from the pregame ceremonies. The starting pitcher sent the ball into the catcher's mitt with a pop. The players prepared their bats with pine tar and rosin. The coaches met with the umpires at home plate. It seemed that everyone knew what they were doing—except me!

A few players stood around in front of the dugout, awaiting the start of the game. Isolated from the masses, I overheard one of the players conversing with two people at the fence. Dressed in black suits and sunglasses, the men did not fit the description of the typical fan. "We have to meet tonight."

"If the game doesn't go into extra innings," the player responded.

"It's very important that you're there," the one on the left insisted. "The boss is getting concerned about your approach."

Scanning into the stands, I listened intently. I did not recognize the player.

"Don't worry about my approach. I'm getting closer and I don't want to blow it," the player said.

"Just know, this has been going on too long."

The player looked toward the outfield. I read the name on the back of his jersey—Thompson. Before the opener, I had studied the team and I did not recall a *Thompson*. Suddenly, the three men looked in my direction. Looking away, I waved to an unknown person in the crowd.

Thompson continued, "You will not …" the crowd noise drowned out his voice, "… again, is that clear?" He turned and started toward me. I bent over and picked up a hot dog wrapper as he walked by, acting as if I did not exist. When I straightened up, the men in suits were gone and Thompson had blended in with the rest of the team.

CHAPTER
2

The interaction of Thompson and the two men in the suits gnawed at me for the first few innings. After a while, I got lost in the game as I got more comfortable with my new batboy role. After the game was over, Mom and Dad came down to see me at the fence along the third base dugout. We chatted for a second, and then they left me to my postgame chores.

I picked up the towels in the dugout and crunched my way over a floor of sunflower seed shells. *I'm so glad I don't have to be the one to clean this mess*, I thought. The grounds crew watered the field and the stadium sat empty. Quietness lingered throughout the structure. The dimmed lights created eerie shadows throughout the steel framework of the retractable roof.

Inside the clubhouse, it was a different story. The players dove into the post game spread, sang in the showers and played cards. It was loud and boisterous as they celebrated their first win of the year. Groans emanated from the training room as players received their postgame treatments. The clanking of weights echoed from the workout room as others finished some extra lifting. Humid air poured out of the shower room and mixed with the odor of beer and food.

The team cleared out leaving me with the unglamorous part of the job—picking up dirty, sweaty clothes. I walked around cleaning up items, grabbing uniforms, t-shirts and even jockstraps, and then threw them into bags. Greg hustled the laundry into his machines so that we could put it back out before we left for the night. I cleaned out the trash and straightened each locker, and then attacked a mound of dirty cleats, polishing them until they looked new. It was close to midnight when I finished. I ran to First Avenue to catch the bus and fell into my bed, exhausted, as soon as I got home.

Arriving at school the next day, I felt like a rock star. It's amazing how many kids knew about my gig. I didn't realize that South Seattle High School had so many students!

"Hey, Van, you got my two tickets for tonight?" asked Fred Jacobs, who was my best friend, and apparently, my new agent. I made the mistake of telling him about the free tickets I got each night. Fred continued, "I've already talked with a ton of the guys and I'm laying out a schedule so that you don't have to deal with this ticket stuff."

"Fred, I don't need you playing agent for me. What's in it for you, are they greasing your palm to get into the ticket pool?"

"Nah, I'm just trying to make life a little easier for you bro, after all, you're a star now and you need to get your posse together."

He meant well. His skinny body stood about the same height as me and his light brown surfer hair matched his cluelessness. He was a good buddy, always looking out for me over the past four years. More than once, he took the blame for something that I did. I guess once your rep wasn't so good, it was better to protect your best friend's rep. At least that way there was always one of us that could be on the good side of the adults.

Someone yanked my arm and as I pulled away, I heard, "So, the big shot is too cool to hang out with me?"

"No way. I didn't even see you," I replied as my cheeks blushed. Zoe smiled at me with her perfect teeth and punched me on the arm.

"You should have texted me after the game last night. I wanted to see how it went," she said as she flipped her wavy blonde hair behind her ear.

"I didn't get home until after midnight and I was dead tired."

I had known Zoe since elementary school. We learned to snowboard together and used to spend a lot of time hiking with our friends and families growing up. She had always seemed like one of the guys.

"So, Zoe, you want to be a part of Van's posse?" my agent asked.

"Posse? Are you kidding me? Van, one day on the job and it's already gone to your head?" Zoe fumed.

"He's crazy," I said. "That's just Fred's way of getting in on the action."

The bell rang and the three of us strolled to first period.

"Hey, did you catch word about the assembly on Friday?" Fred asked.

"What assembly?" Zoe and I asked in unison.

"Dude, you should totally know. You're the main attraction. They want you to talk to the school about how you got the job. The superintendent is even coming to get pictures with you."

"You're totally nuts, Fred. I haven't heard anything about this."

"I have sources everywhere. You should know that. It's how I stay out of trouble. Anyway, I'm stoked 'cause we're getting out of sixth period for this, so you better do it."

As we arrived at our first class, the principal, Mrs. Silvernail, waited outside the door.

"Van, do you have a moment to speak?" she asked.

Okay—so Fred was right. As it turned out, there was an assembly scheduled for Friday. Mrs. Silvernail had all the details in place. The rest of the day, I managed to get through my classes without too much fanfare and couldn't wait to get back to the ballpark.

CHAPTER
3

During my second day in the clubhouse, I felt like I had been there forever. Before the game, I walked onto the field, looked into the stands and saw Fred. It was an hour and a half before game time and he was already there.

"Hey, Van," he shouted loud enough for the few people around him to see that he knew me, "can you hook me up with an autographed ball or something?"

"Fred, just chill. You know I can't." I didn't blame him for trying and I tossed him a bag of sunflower seeds as a consolation prize.

"Thanks, Van. You know, you almost look like a ballplayer in that uniform, has anybody asked you for an autograph yet?" As if on cue, a small boy ran past Fred and stuck his program out. "Hey, Mister, can I have your autograph?"

"No, kid, I'm just the batboy, you don't really want my autograph."

After watching the kid slink away, Fred said, "Dude, what's wrong with you, I can't believe you didn't sign it for him. He would've never known!"

"I can't do that to some kid. He'll be looking at his program all night trying to figure out who signed it."

"I'm just saying. Wouldn't it be fun to sign some balls?"

"Fred, I've got to go pick up in the dugout. Why don't you go meet some girls?"

"Have you looked around tonight? This place is loaded!"

Scanning the stands, I noticed a smattering of fans. I walked away shaking my head.

In the dugout, I picked up some towels, turned toward the clubhouse and crashed into Ron Cantos, the best player on the team and a perennial all-star. He also had a reputation of being one of the meanest players in the majors, and not a very good "clubhouse guy."

"Watch it, batboy!"

"Sorry, Ron, I didn't see you there," I said, as I crept back, out of the way.

"Well, you better look out. You won't be working here long if you keep crashing into the players. Here's the way it's gonna be. I go where I want. You stay out of my way. The next time you get in my way, you better look out because I'll flatten you. And if you go crying to your boss, I'll just say, 'I didn't see you.'" He marched into the clubhouse without looking back.

I grabbed more towels and tried to disappear behind them. Inside, the players dug into the pregame snack of watermelon, grapes and apples. I retreated to my locker and wondered how many players were like Cantos. I hoped not too many.

Looking across the room, I noticed Thompson sitting at his locker. I looked him up last night, and he didn't have a career that would impress anyone. It was no wonder I didn't know about him. Cantos walked in and stopped at his locker. Thompson gave him a quick glance, from his adjoining locker. Although their body types were similar, there couldn't be two more opposite players. Everyone knew Cantos and hardly anybody had heard of Thompson. Cantos was loud, crude and one of the best players around. Thompson was quiet, perfectly groomed and a below average ballplayer. In fact, Thompson didn't even look like a ballplayer. He was jittery and was always reading newspapers, which littered the floor around his locker.

"Van!" shouted Ricky, one of the clubhouse attendants, or "clubbie" as the ballplayers called them. "You can't sit there and stare at the players. Get up and keep moving. There's plenty to do. If Greg catches you sitting around, he'll go ballistic. Go pick up that pile of newspapers over by Thompson. See if anyone needs more polish on their shoes."

Ricky Carney had been a clubbie for three years, so he knew the ropes. He was a couple of years older than I was and knew many of the players. Taking his advice, I headed over to the pile of newspapers and started picking them up.

"Don't touch those!" screamed Thompson. The entire clubhouse went quiet for a split second. He continued, quieter and without emotion, in a staccato-like cadence, "I haven't read those. Here, you can take these away."

I stood frozen for a moment. *What's his problem*, I wondered. The clubhouse noise returned to its normal level as the teammates continued with their pregame business. I threw the papers in the recycling bucket and watched Thompson out of the corner of my eye. Jumpy and constantly looking around, he reminded me of an animal protecting his food stores. Clearly, he was out-of-sync with this environment.

"Hey, Ricky, what's up with Thompson? That guy is kind of weird, don't you think?"

"Van, the first thing you have to learn is that ballplayers are a different breed. They have all kinds of superstitions and rituals. If you mess that up, you are in big trouble. Our job is to be in the background and stay out of their way. Just hang with me and you'll see how I do it."

The good news was that Ricky was a good guy and I could learn from him. The bad news was—I had a lot to learn.

CHAPTER
4

The night went by quickly, a pitcher's duel that took less than two hours. Cantos belted two home runs and looked to be off to a fast start, although that didn't change his attitude much. After one of his home runs, he walked up to give me his batting helmet and just as I reached out to grab it, he dropped it to the ground. *What a jerk.*

I still couldn't figure out Mark Thompson. He always sat at the end of the bench with no other players around him. When in the lineup, he played a decent second base, with a little bat and okay defense, certainly not all-star quality. The loner never talked to any of the other ballplayers.

We finished the clubhouse chores early and I was home before midnight. I wasn't ready for sleep, so I picked up a shoebox full of baseball cards and sifted through them. I pulled out some of the players that I had worked with over the past two days. Johnson, Smith and, of course, Cantos, were in my collection. The Angels were in next, so I stacked their cards, looking forward to a new group of players.

The Moe Berg card from Dad sat on the nightstand. Picking it up, I looked at his stats. He was an average player and never made any All-Star teams. If Dad thought this card was special, then I did too. I propped it up against my lamp on the nightstand then drifted off for some much needed sleep.

I was up early and ready for school in minutes. Bounding down the stairs, I stopped at the kitchen door. "Hi, Dad," I said with a surprised look.

"Hey, sport, how was your second day on the job?"

"It was awesome! Cantos went yard twice. I'm getting into the routine now. The night just flew by. Who would think that I could have so much fun picking up jock straps?"

"How are the other guys who work in the clubhouse?"

"They're okay, this kid Ricky has been around for a few years and he's showing me the ropes. My boss has been in baseball for about thirty years. He doesn't seem too happy most of the time, but all in all, it's not so bad. So, why are you home this morning?" I asked.

"That's a good question. I've been working on a project recently and for some reason, they put it on hold. Some of the higher-ups emailed and asked me to back off for a while—take a couple of weeks off. So, here I am!"

"That's cool, are you going to be able to catch a couple of ballgames now?" I asked.

"You bet, but I don't want to take away from your friends getting to the games. I hear you have quite the following now."

"Oh, yeah, Fred's become my *manager*," I replied with the two-finger quotation mark thing. "It'll be great to have you around for the next couple of weeks. Well, I have to get to school. I'll catch you later, Dad."

Mom entered the room with a tired look on her face. "Have fun at school, Van. This weekend you'll have to tell us all about your new job."

"Sure thing, Mom, gotta run." Mom didn't appear too concerned about Dad being home. She was lucky because she didn't have to work—well, at least not at an office or anything. I suppose it was a lot of work taking care of Dad and me.

How often does someone take time off in the middle of a project, I thought, while walking to school. He got time off, but we usually knew about it ahead of time and planned a vacation or something. As a scientist, he worked on some very cutting edge, cool stuff. Mostly quantum physics and nanotechnologies, it was all very secretive. During his college years, he blew up lots of things, not necessarily on purpose. Now he worked for a private company, Biotrust. I had been to his office a couple of times, but not since moving into their new facility.

Although he was gone a bunch, he was a great dad and I loved him. We had many great times camping, taking road trips, watching baseball and just plain hanging out. I knew that he loved me too, although he didn't show it too often. He was mellow and didn't get too emotional. When I would ask him what he was working on at Biotrust, he would usually give me some vague answer and quickly change the subject. Most of the time, I would just let it go and enjoy my time with him.

Spring was trying to take over winter as the thermometer inched up a couple of degrees. When I arrived at school, Zoe was waiting for me and I didn't like the look on her face.

"Hey, bigshot. When do *I* get to go to a game? I can't wait to see you out there in your uniform," she said sarcastically.

"Come on, Zoe, you don't have to embarrass me like that."

"Lighten up, Van. I'm just messing with you."

"I know, it's just—everyone is asking for tickets."

"Am I just *everyone*?"

"You know you're not, I can't wait for you to come to a game. Can you make it tonight?"

From out of nowhere, Fred crashed into the two of us. "Yeah, that'll be great! Zoe and I will be there right as the gates open. I don't want to miss batting practice."

"Ugh, do *you* have to go too? I get enough of you around here and now I have to go to a ballgame with you?" Zoe said, sticking her finger down her throat.

"Are you kidding? It'll be awesome. I promise I won't embarrass you by starting the wave. Let me check my vitals and see if I booked the tickets for anyone else," Fred said as he pulled out his iPhone and checked the calendar.

"What if I gave them away already?" I asked.

"Van, I know that you haven't even had time to breathe. That's why I'm your manager and posse rolled into one. Don't worry. You won't have to bother with those pesky tickets again."

"Pesky tickets? You're one of a kind, Fred."

"So, what's it really like in the locker room?" Zoe asked.

"Well, it's more than a locker room, that's why we call it a clubhouse. It's really decked out with just about everything you need. All the food and drink you could want, Xbox, TV's, couches, you name it."

"So," Fred asked, "when can you get me in for a look?"

"What do you mean, get you in. Are you crazy? Do you remember Pete Rose? Well, after his little gambling problem, the league adopted the 'Pete Rose Rule.' Nobody gets in without being a part of the team or the media."

"Maybe I should request a media pass from our school newspaper," Fred said while Zoe and I both rolled our eyes. "Nah, that's okay. I think I'd rather sit in the stands, checking out the girls. I sure hope it gets warm soon. That's when the scenery gets *really* nice."

"You're pathetic, Fred," Zoe said. "C'mon, we have to get to class."

CHAPTER
5

That afternoon, I rode Metro Transit to the ballpark. The player's bus arrived just as I did and because it was "get-away-day," the entire team was on it. Today, we would pack up the player's duffel bags and then load the team's equipment onto the truck as soon as the game ended.

Out on the field, I was picking up the bats after batting practice, when out of the corner of my eye, I saw Cantos walking toward me. *There's no escape,* I thought. *What's it going to be this time?*

"Yo, batboy, what's your name?"

"Who me?"

"Yeah, you. You're the batboy, aren't you?"

"It's Van—Van Stone," I replied.

"Well, it's nice to meet you, Van, and I wanted you to know that you've done a good job this series. I know how tough it can be with the crowds and the superstars. It's a little overwhelming. Just keep doing what you're doing and you'll be fine," Cantos said.

I stood there stunned. *What happened to this guy?* Maybe the two dingers he hit last night put him in a good mood. "Thanks—Ron."

"So, what grade you in?"

"I'm a sophomore at South Seattle High."

"Do you play ball for your school?"

"I did last year, but not this year. With this gig, it didn't make much sense. Besides, it's not like I was going to go to the majors on my skills," I said.

"How'd you get interested in baseball?"

"My dad was always into it and I would come to games with him. I also collect baseball cards. I learned a lot about the players that way."

"Do you have any of me?" Cantos asked.

"Actually, I do, I was looking at them last night."

"Bring them in next time I'm in town and I'll sign them for you," he offered. "Here, rub some good luck on my gamer," Cantos said as he handed me his bat.

I took it from him not knowing what to do. I tapped the barrel twice. "Good luck tonight," I said. *Good luck tonight, I couldn't come up with something better than that?* How lame. It didn't matter. Now I belonged to an exclusive club. The rest of the night, I was flying high in the club known as Major League baseball.

The game ended and there was a mad rush to get the team packed up and out the door. Dirty laundry went straight into bags and shipped for the next clubhouse to unpack and wash. Crates were loaded with the equipment and hauled to the truck outside the clubhouse door. Instead of the usual fun and laid-back atmosphere, the players showered, dressed and climbed aboard the bus for their trip to the airport.

The clubhouse was bustling. I watched as Greg hustled through the room with a bank money pouch from 1955, collecting the clubhouse dues. Suddenly, the first baseman, Rick Robins, tapped me on the shoulder and handed me a twenty-dollar bill. "Thanks, batboy," he said.

"Uh, sure, Rick—no problem," I said with a shocked look. A few more ballplayers came up, handing me various amounts. Ten bucks here, more twenties—this kept going on throughout the night as the players dressed and left the clubhouse. No one had told me about this part of the job. It was great!

Cantos walked up and said, "Here you go, Van. I'll see you next time, and don't forget to bring those cards in for me to sign." I looked down and stared at a hundred dollar bill in my hand.

"Thanks, Ron. Have a great season!" I replied. *Have a great season*? I had to stop saying such lame things. He was the last one out, so I walked to my locker and emptied my tips into my backpack. I had scored over three hundred bucks.

The empty clubhouse sat cluttered and trashed, with the unmistakable smell of stale beer. The humidity hung thick, as if a new weather system had formed in the clubhouse. The smell of burgers and fries called to me. I devoured mine sitting on cloud nine.

"Hey, Van, how did you make out tonight?" asked Ricky.

"I did great. How come you didn't tell me about the tips?"

"Seriously, if you had known, you would've been kissing their butts. It's better for you to get to know the job first, before finding out you could make a little extra cash," Ricky said. "Now that you know, just be careful. Don't be thinking about the money, that's not why we're here. We love the game of baseball. We're one of a handful of kids, across the country that work in a clubhouse. If that's not a good enough reason to be here, then you probably shouldn't be."

"No way, Ricky, I would do this job for free. You can't beat it, but the tips sure are nice!"

Greg disappeared as soon as the team left. As usual, he didn't seem to be in a very good mood. He started in on his chores, without sitting down to eat anything. Walking by, he glared at us as we ate, mumbling under his breath.

After we finished, Ricky took charge. "Start with the lockers. Trash everything you find, unless it's something personal that a ballplayer might have left behind. When you're done with a locker, pull down the nameplate. I'll start with the showers and bathrooms."

Moving from locker to locker, I tossed athletic tape, dry cleaning wrappers and empty boxes from whatever it was they spent their millions. Each locker told a story about the player, some didn't have a thing in them and for others—it was as if they had lived in it for three days.

Rick Robins' locker was empty, so I pulled down his nameplate. Next was Cantos. What a slob. Half-full beers, a plate with scraps of a burger, magazines, empty shoeboxes and enough athletic tape to wrap a mummy—I tossed it all in the garbage.

I moved over to Thompson's locker. Spotless. I climbed up and checked out the shelf where I found a couple of scraps from a newspaper and some kind of strange looking plastic thing. Looking at the scraps, I saw a row of letters and numbers. I recognized that it was the listings for local companies. Highlighted on each scrap were the letters BIOT, the stock symbol for Biotrust.

I examined the plastic thing. It was the size of two baseball cards side by side. It probably belonged to some kid who wanted his cards signed and Thompson forgot to send it back with the cards. I threw the holder in my backpack, took down his nameplate and started on the next locker.

Greg stormed around the lockers and looked right at me. "What are you doing? It's taking you forever to get these lockers done. We don't have all night and we have another ballclub coming in tonight."

My faced turned red instantly as the guilt ran through my veins. "I'm sorry. I didn't ..."

"I don't want to hear it. Get back to work," Greg interrupted.

I hurried through the rest of the lockers and didn't give a second thought about what I threw out. Just as I finished, I heard the Angels' equipment truck pull up outside the main door. I walked back to the washroom to tell Greg. His enormous heft pressed against the washing machine while he polished them as if it was an antique car. I had never seen anybody so obsessed with having a shiny washer and dryer. His balding head sweated profusely as he stood on a step stool trying to clean the farthest reaches.

"Greg, the truck's here," I said.

He stumbled down and slammed shut a door from the cabinet attached to the opposite wall. In a fluid movement, he slapped a padlock to the cabinet and screamed, "Don't sneak up on me like that ever again. You better watch it rookie, or you won't be here much longer."

"Sorry, I didn't mean to. Ricky told me to come get you." I slinked away and scrambled to the front door.

Ricky threw open the doors and locked them into place, the diesel exhaust filled the entryway. We unloaded trunks, sorted the player's equipment bags and the laundry headed to the shiny washer and dryer. Within forty-five minutes, every locker looked like it was fresh out of a catalogue. The uniforms hung in front of each locker, the cleats polished to perfection, lined up with toes out, sat like soldiers at attention. As I looked around the room, I was amazed at the transformation that had occurred.

Ricky and I walked out together, talking about the Angels. He waited with me until I boarded Metro Transit. I chose a seat right behind the bus driver. It was after midnight, when a more diverse crowd rode, or slept, on the bus. I looked toward the back and saw a dirty, unshaven kid drinking out of a brown paper bag, a man mumbling and a woman looking into space, apparently talking on her Bluetooth, hidden beneath her shaggy rust colored hair. The stale urine stench attacked my nostrils. *I need a car as soon as possible*, I thought.

When I got home, I showered away the bus ride and went to my room. As I lay on the bed, I grabbed a box of baseball cards. Taking two out, I checked the new holder. Just as I thought, two cards fit, side by side. Examining the holder, I observed a metallic border on the inside ridge.

Rolling over, I booted up my laptop and searched the *Beckett's* site, looking for any new types of cards. The card companies were always trying new things like holograms, gold plated, ceramic and the like, so maybe I could find something about this new holder. After about a half hour, I gave up. No trace of it. I powered down and hit the sack just after 1:30 a.m.

CHAPTER
6

I woke up with that Friday kind of anticipation. Buzzing with energy, I got dressed and couldn't wait to get the day started. After school, it was off to the ballpark and then the weekend would be here, when I could practically live at the stadium.

I walked into the kitchen and smelled the warm, greasy odor of frying bacon. Mom slid two eggs onto a plate and cracked two more into a sizzling pan.

"Van, you sure did get in late last night," Mom pointed out.

"The Angels' stuff came in after the game, so it did take a little longer than usual. Don't worry. It's only going to be that late once or twice every home stand—or if the game goes into extra innings."

"I'm really worried about you taking the bus that late, maybe next time you should call us and we can come pick you up," she said.

Dad jumped to my defense. "Oh, come on, honey. He's a big boy. He can handle himself just fine on the bus, right, Van?"

"Well, it is a little creepy," I said, setting up for the big one. "What I really need is a car so I wouldn't have to bother you guys. Last night I made over three hundred bucks in tips! Pretty sweet, huh? If this keeps up, I might be able to get something by the end of May."

"A car! I don't know, Van, that's a little drastic," Mom said. "First, you're this big 'Major Leaguer' and now you want to be 'hot-rodding' around in your own car. What's it going to be next, do you want meal money and an expense account?"

"Go easy on him, Linda, when I was Van's age all I could think about was a car," Dad said, coming to my rescue. "I'm not saying he needs to run out and get one, but it might be something to think about."

Wow, is it possible that he could he on my side on this one? I wondered. Looking at Mom, she hid the emotion on her face behind her long brown hair. The eggs turned from over easy to well done as she regained her composure.

"I'm not saying no, but we have to talk more about this. It scares me that you're growing up so fast. All this big league attention and talk about cars, I don't know ..."

"Don't worry, Mom. I only want a car so that it will be easier on you guys, and you won't have to worry about me late at night," I said unconvincingly.

Dad jumped in and said, "You're right, Linda. We should talk about this some more. In the meantime, it can't hurt to research what is out there. It definitely won't be happening overnight."

"Even if we were to consider this, there would be strict ground rules about the use of the car," Mom said.

"I think Van would agree with that, right?"

"Sure," I said as my excitement grew.

"And your grades, if your grades start to slip, no more car," Mom negotiated.

"You got it. You won't see my grades budge except in the upward direction," I replied.

"Let's all go look around when the team's on the road and see what's out there. Meanwhile, Van, you should start looking at the *Seattle Times*, Craigslist and even eBay. I know someone who bought an RX-7 on eBay. Can you believe that? Now, we're not saying you're getting something right away, but at least we'll have an idea about what's out there."

My heart was racing. I didn't think it would be so easy. "That's great guys, sounds like a plan. Don't worry, Mom, you can trust me." I practically inhaled my overcooked eggs, then said, "Thanks for the great breakfast."

"Hey, sport, are you leaving us tickets for tonight or do we have to pay to see you in action?" Dad asked.

"Sure, you can have them. If Fred already promised them to somebody then he'll have to buy tickets," I said. "See you tonight—come see me on the field before the game."

On the way to school, I hopped into the AM/PM Mini Mart and picked up an *Auto Trader*. Arriving at school, I walked into the main hall. Tons of students banged the lockers, fired up about weekend plans. Fred stood by my locker.

"What's with you? Are you camping out here waiting for me to walk in the door?" I asked, carrying the *Auto Trader* so he would see it.

"Whoa, Van. Are you getting a car? That's tight!" Fred screamed. "What happened, did you win the lottery last night? Did you sign a Major League contract? If you got the contract, remember, I get fifteen percent as your agent."

"Come on, Fred, chill out, I didn't win anything, but I did get THREE HUNDRED BUCKS IN TIPS!" *I couldn't help myself.* "I'm thinking about getting a car so I don't have to keep taking the bus."

"That would be money! Think about all the things that we could do if you scored a car. We could cruise through downtown on the weekends, maybe head over to Alki and hang at the beach. What kind of car do you want? I think you should go with something practical, like a convertible."

I looked down the hall and saw Zoe coming toward us. She wore jeans and a spring-like shirt, which hinted that summer was getting closer. The kind of shirt that wasn't summery, but showed more skin than I had seen all winter. A sudden jolt of adrenalin rushed through me. *Whoa, what was that?* That was *not* supposed to happen.

"Hi, Zoe, bet you're glad it's Friday?" another brilliant comment uttered from my mouth.

"You got that right. What kind of trouble are you guys getting into?"

"Zoe, Van's buying a car," Fred said.

"Fred, just relax. No, Zoe, I'm *looking* for a car so I don't have to keep taking the bus in the middle of the night. I'm making some good money in tips at the ballpark."

"Wow, I didn't know that you could make that kind of money in the clubhouse. I thought it was all about the experience and hanging with the ballplayers. I imagine that as soon as you get a car, you'll be off in another world, a high roller, living the life. You'll forget all about us little people."

"No way, Zoe. After I get my car we can go out for pizza or something, maybe a movie?"

"Van Stone, did you just ask me out on a date?"

"Well, not really, I just thought it would be cool to hang out." *I have to do something about my blushing problem.*

Fred jumped in, "Slow down there, Zoe. Van and I will be heading out to Alki and if you're really nice, maybe we'll invite you too."

"Zip it, Fred. I can handle my own social calendar. Zoe, don't hold your breath on any of this, it'll be a couple of months before I can even afford a car. I'm just kicking some tires now."

The day dragged as it approached the dreaded sixth period assembly. I walked into the gym and saw the entire school gathered for the event. Nervously, I walked across the floor staring at tons of lights, two stools and cables strewn everywhere. Mrs. Silvernail approached, "Van, I would like to introduce you to John Marks, from *Channel 13*. He's here to conduct the interview today."

"*Channel 13*? You didn't mention anything about TV."

"Isn't it lovely? We got the call yesterday. Apparently, your story has been creating quite the buzz and they're taping for a special news piece. Aren't you *thrilled*, you're going to be on *TV*!"

My palms went liquid as I looked at the man with a camera on his shoulder.

"Hi, Van, just relax and be yourself," Marks said.

"If I was being myself, I wouldn't be here. This isn't my kind of thing," I replied.

"C'mon, you'll be fine. Let's get started," Marks said. We moved to the stools under the beam of the stage lights. After a brief introduction, the interviewer asked the first question, "Van, tell us a little about how you got the job."

I hesitated, looking at the front row of students. "Well, I wrote an essay on why I wanted to be a batboy." The heat of the lights bombarded my face, eliciting beads of sweat. I fought the urge to wipe it away.

"What happened next?"

Fred sat three rows deep and held a big sign that read "DON'T LAUGH". Stifling a crack up, I looked away. "Well, out of hundreds of essays, the *Seattle Times* narrowed the submissions down to ten essays."

"Wow, that's a lot of competition," John said with his best Joe Buck impersonation. "So, tell us about the interviews."

"Um, there's not really that much to tell, except that I was probably as nervous then—as I am now." Laughter rolled through the crowd. I continued, struggling to convey my experience, "I went through four interviews and was ecstatic each time I was called back. It finally dwindled to two possibilities and, well, here I am."

"That sounds pretty exciting. When did you know that you had it in the bag?" Marks asked with a toothy, bleached smile.

"Never, you should have seen the other guys. They always looked so prepared and comfortable—they looked like they came right out of a catalogue."

Marks delivered one of his trademark fake laughs and asked, "What's your favorite thing so far?"

"Ah, that's a tough question. There are so many great things—" And so it went for the next thirty minutes, followed by handshakes and photos. When it ended, I was relieved to have the focus off me and couldn't wait to get back to the ballpark.

CHAPTER
7

Due to the assembly, I arrived late to the clubhouse. Walking in, I heard the now familiar sounds of players shouting in Spanish, the groans of someone losing in Xbox and the clanging of weights that never seems to stop. The new team occupying the space slowly destroyed the perfectly neat scene from last night.

Eric Cooper, their star third baseman, walked right up to me. "Clubbie, I rang up some wings for delivery. Here's a twenty for 'em. Can you keep an eye out? Thanks."

It was his routine every day. He ate chicken before every ballgame.

"Sure, no problem," I said. After changing, I walked out to the security gate.

"Hey, Charlie, can you call into the clubhouse when the wing delivery comes in for Eric Cooper?"

"Sure, Van, no problem. How's it going for you after your first series?"

"Great, I feel like I've been here for years already."

"How 'bout the players? Everybody treating you okay?"

"Yeah, pretty much. Cantos started out like a jerk, but he got nice at the end. That Mark Thompson guy was really strange."

"Yeah, I noticed that too. You have to watch yourself sometimes. These million dollar athletes think they can get away with anything."

"I will, and thanks for your advice." I ran back into the clubhouse. Ten minutes later, Charlie called and I went out to fetch the wings.

"Here you go, kid," Charlie said.

"Where did the delivery guy go?" I asked.

"He had to run. I paid the guy for the wings."

"How much were they, all I have with me is a twenty."

"It was fifteen bucks, including tip, but don't worry about it," Charlie said.

"Really? But that's not right."

"Like I said, don't worry about it. I'm sure you'll get a chance to take care of me one day."

Back in the clubhouse, Cooper waited anxiously for his wings. "Ah, that's what I'm waiting for, that Wings N' Things place is so dope. I get 'em from there every time I come to town." I handed him the bag. "Keep the change, kid," he said. The day was starting great.

On the field, it was a typical Seattle day, overcast with a marine breeze, making it feel more like February than April. The retractable roof was open, nonetheless. I looked up at the engineering marvel that made it worth the trip to Safeco Field by itself. It weighed twenty-two million pounds and sat on 128 massive steel wheels that rolled the roof out over the field. Even with the roof closed, you experienced an open-air feeling in the stadium. Its highest point soared 215 feet above the field. Today, it sat folded back over the train yard, amplifying the frequent horn blasts.

The fans trickled in on this Friday night. There should be a big crowd with the archrival Angels in town. I spotted my parents at the railing in the stands and jogged over to them, attracting a swarm of kids.

"Can you sign this?"

"Hey, Mister, sign my ball, please?"

Six kids shoved their arms out with pens.

"I'm just the batboy," I repeated for the hundredth time in the last few days. The group frowned, except for one kid, who yelled, "Can you get me Eric Cooper's autograph?"

"You'll have to ask him when he comes in from batting practice."

"Looks like you have a fan club," Dad said. Mom chimed in, "You look so cute in your uniform, let me take your picture." She tried to snap a shot. The camera remained off, because she had it on the wrong setting.

Dad grabbed the Canon. "Let me see, I think it needs to be on this little green thingy here," he said, fumbling with the buttons.

"No, I think that's for the video. Oh, no, you're right. It is the little green thingy."

My dad, the great scientist, was talking about the little green thingy. Looking into the stands, I felt self-conscious, as the fans followed the comedic routine. Finally, I heard a click as the flash exploded.

"Van, you weren't looking at the camera! Let's do it again," Mom said. "Smile ..." I saw spots in my eyes as the flash popped again.

"Got it. Oh, no—Van, you had one of your eyes closed," she said.

"Mom, close enough. You're embarrassing me."

"How is the team compared to Oakland?" Dad asked.

"They're pretty good so far. I had to take care of Cooper's chicken superstition. I also talked to a couple of the guys about Seattle and where to go for some good food. They seem a lot more relaxed than the last group."

"Maybe that's because they win the division almost every year," Dad replied.

"Oh, you guys, stop talking baseball, you can do that over the weekend," Mom interrupted. "Are you getting enough to eat, did you have dinner yet? Who is the grumpy looking guy over there wearing the white outfit in the dugout? Where's the young boy that you said works with you? What was his name—Ricky?"

"Mom, cut it out. First, I usually don't eat until after the game. Secondly, the guy over in the dugout is my boss, so I wouldn't talk too loud about him, and third, yes—*Ricky* is probably in the clubhouse, which is where I should be now that BP is over."

"BP—what's that? Are you trying to get all NASA on me so I don't know what you're talking about?"

"BP is batting practice, jeez, Mom, what's wrong with you tonight?" I asked.

"Don't worry, Van, she's been like this all day. I don't think she's used to having someone around all the time. I'll get her a hot chocolate and some peanuts and she'll be fine."

"I *am* just fine. *This* guy," Mom said while pointing at Dad with her thumb, "is like my shadow. He's bored out of his mind. Let's go get that hot chocolate, it is somewhat chilly today. Bye, Van, have a great game. I love you," Mom shouted as Dad pulled her arm to take her up to the concourse.

"Bye, see you later," I answered. Watching them walk up the steps, I realized how proud they were of me. I was lucky—I had great parents, a great job that almost any kid would want and great friends. As they approached the concourse, I noticed two men sitting near the railing. They were the same two guys from the first night, wearing the same suits and sunglasses. The one on the right looked at a Mariners' program and the other texted on his phone. I had an uneasy feeling that they had been watching our entire exchange. I supposed they could be season ticket holders that come straight from work, but I couldn't shake the feeling that it was more than just that.

I jogged to the dugout where Ricky stood with a smirk. "How was the photo shoot?"

"You saw that? I was so embarrassed. Those were my parents."

"No kidding, I thought they might be your extremely old step brother and sister. Of course, it was your parents. Just as a warning, we have a kangaroo court in here every week or so. If I catch you doing stupid things like that, we'll fine you. It's okay to talk to people, but if you're 'dorking' out to a photo shoot, that's worthy of a fine. I'll let you slide this time, rookie, you better watch it in the future."

We walked together into the clubhouse that had taken a more serious turn as it neared game time. A quiet calm enveloped the room and a few players whispered. The attitude and professionalism with this group exceeded anything I had experienced with the last team. After changing into my game uniform, I returned to the field. There was a capacity crowd tonight and I felt the energy in the ballpark.

Looking for my parents, I stepped out onto the warning track. Sitting in the ballplayer's family section, I saw Mom sipping her hot chocolate, talking with some of the player's wives. Dad sat next to her, looking through the program and writing in the starting lineup so that he could keep score. Seeing them reminded me of how cool this experience had been and how my life had changed in a matter of a few weeks.

The game was a classic. A pitcher's duel ensued for the first seven innings and then the bats came out. The crowd was electric, cheering at every strikeout and fly ball. I kept looking up at Dad in the stands and I could tell he was in seventh heaven. It was a great reward for him, a little time off and enjoying one of the great passions in his life.

The Angels won with a come-from-behind victory. The clubhouse turned into a zoo after the game. As I walked to my locker, music transported me from salsa, to meringue, to metal, to country, to hip-hop and finally rap, all within the space of about forty feet. The players showered and rushed out to experience the nightlife of Seattle. Ricky and I hurried through our post game chores and we walked out together, leaving the clubhouse with its little soldiers lined up in each locker, toes pointed out.

CHAPTER
8

Saturday finally arrived. I had always liked school, but recently, it had become somewhat of a distraction. I was a good student. However, I was finding that I could hardly wait to get to the ballpark. I ate a quick bagel and packed my backpack to leave when Dad yelled from the family room, "Van, you want to go out and toss the ball around for a bit? I've never played ball with a major leaguer before."

"Sure, Dad, I've got some time. Do you remember how? I haven't seen you play catch in about five years."

"I'll show you, rookie. I'll give you one of my 'Jack Specials' and see if you can handle the bottom falling out. Grab your glove and let's go."

The next hour was one of my favorite times in years. I couldn't remember the last time we got to hang out like that. Minutes ago, I couldn't wait to get to the clubhouse and now I didn't want this moment to end. There was something special about tossing the ball around with your dad. Any number of activities—like constructing a tree house, fixing a lawn mower engine or building a model, felt the same way. At that isolated moment in time, nothing else in the world existed.

I missed a couple of "Jack Specials" to make Dad feel good, like he still "had it." Too soon, our time ended.

"Forget the bus. I'll drop you off today," Dad said. I retrieved my bag and we jumped into his car. "Are you getting tired of me being around so much?"

"It's been great, Dad, too bad you can't do this all the time."

"Well, actually, I've been thinking about leaving Biotrust. I could open a consulting company and work from home. We could spend more time together. What do you think about that?"

"That would be awesome!"

"I've been talking to your mom about it. She thinks it's a good idea, too. I just hope I don't drive her crazy by working from home."

"I know she's been acting all weird lately, but with my new gig at the ballpark and with you being home, there's a lot more testosterone flying around. So—you really think you're going to do it?" I asked.

"I think so. We shouldn't have any trouble with the startup. I have many relationships that might lead to business right away. The more I think about it, the more excited I get."

Dad looked like a kid in a candy store. His enthusiasm bubbled to the surface.

"Here we are, Van, the limousine has arrived. Have fun today and I'll see you in the morning. I'm sure I'll be in bed when you get home tonight."

"Thanks for the ride." I jumped out and walked to the gate.

The day was magnificent—it was hard to imagine that they used to play baseball indoors, in the concrete mushroom known as the Kingdome. As always, Charlie manned the security gate.

"Hi'ya, Van. Who's that dropping you off?" he asked.

"Hi, Charlie, that's my dad," I said proudly.

"He must be one lucky father."

"I think I'm one lucky kid," I said as I spun through the turnstile.

In the clubhouse, I turned the corner and found Greg sitting in the laundry room. He quickly shuffled some papers and threw them into the cabinet, slamming the door shut.

"What do you want?" he barked.

"Nothing, I just wanted to let you know I was here."

"Good, go see if any of the ballplayers need anything."

I walked to my locker wondering what was in the cabinet. While changing into my practice jersey, Eric Cooper strolled up to me. "Yo, clubbie, will you hook me up with some chicken?" he asked.

"Sure, what'll it be this time?" I responded.

He thought for a moment and continued, "How 'bout you choose it for me today—something tight!"

Whoa, my cheeks flushed red and I felt that unmistakable creepy feeling as it climbed up my back. This had to be my most important task all day! Forget the on field, game-time batboy duties, never mind the post game spread—Eric wanted me to pick his pregame superstitious chicken meal. What if I got him a grilled chicken sandwich and he went hitless today. I could see the headlines tomorrow—*Batboy's Choice ends Cooper's Fifteen Game Hitting Streak*. On the other hand, if I got him some Cajun chicken fingers and he went four-for-four with five RBI and a homer. Yeah, that was what I would do, Cajun chicken fingers was just the right call.

I scurried out of the clubhouse with Eric's twenty in my hand. "Hey, Van, you just got here. Where are you headed?" Charlie asked as I jumped past him.

"Eric Cooper is having me pick his pregame chicken. He better have a good day today!"

The crowd was sparse, if you can even call it that, wandering around the gate at this early hour in the day. There was the usual assortment of groupies and graphies, all waiting for their chance for a brush with greatness. Each had their own idea of what that meant. The groupies, let's just say they wanted to hang out. The graphies, they stood around with their notebooks of baseball cards and other assorted items waiting for autographs.

"Dude, when is Eric Cooper getting in?" one of the regulars shouted at me.

There was no way I could tell him I was picking up Cooper's pregame chicken. "He's already inside, better luck tomorrow," I said and continued across the street.

Outside the stadium, I felt the energy that built before a game. Entire cities of tents and vendors popped up where nothing existed before. I heard the screech of the trains in the distance. Inhaling the smell of the street vendor buffet of polish sausages, bratwurst, hotdogs, pork kabobs and roasted peanuts, it brought me back to my days before I was a part of the scene. There was nothing like that smell—mix in a dash of wetness from the morning dew with that familiar vinegar-like rank of standing water, and you had the perfect ballpark experience.

I blasted through the door of an Occidental Avenue eatery. "Hey, Van, whachta havin' today?" asked Vinnie, the owner and apparently the only employee of Wings N' Things. The former New Yorker had been a diehard Mariners' fan since the early years.

"Give me your best Cajun chicken fingers, please. They're for Eric Cooper with the Angels."

"Eric Cooper, that bum! I think I'll add a little extra chili pepper to the mix, special for him." Vinnie dropped the breaded specialties into the hot oil. The sound of water and oil meeting gave off the familiar cacophony of firecracker-like noises. "That guy has been killing us lately, treating our pitchers like it was batting practice."

I threw down Cooper's twenty.

"Don't worry about it, Van. You'll be bringing enough business in here, this one's on me!"

"Wow, thanks, Vinnie. I'll see you tomorrow."

With the goods in my hand, I ran out the door into the street that had filled with more fans and curious seekers. The heat poured through the bag as Charlie opened the security gate. The growing crowd outside watched as I ran through the gate wearing my practice jersey. At the oddest times, I got the feeling that I was one of the luckiest kids in the world.

Back in the clubhouse, I nervously gave the Cajun fingers to Eric. Waiting for a response, I handed him the twenty.

Eric didn't even look at the money, and said. "Keep the change, kid."

In my first fifteen minutes, I had already scored twenty bucks. This was going to be a good day.

Suddenly, Eric screamed, "*Yeeowwww*—what is this stuff, my tongue is on fire!"

"Fajun kitchen chingers, I mean Cajun chicken fingers," I said frantically.

Eric flicked his wrists making his fingers snap. "This is the meanest stuff I've ever had! Clubbie, this stuff is sick. You scored big, now you better hope I have a good game tonight!"

"Uh, thanks," I responded as I retreated to my locker, praying for him to have a great game.

The game crawled along. Both pitchers worked slower than a turtle. After the great game last night, errors dominated tonight's game. My eyes glanced at the clock. Only forty-five minutes had gone by and it felt like hours. The crowd was out of it too, it was more like a ballet audience than baseball fans.

Two more errors and a hit batsman later, I looked up at the time. Nine o'clock. It was only the bottom of the third. This was going to be a long night.

Between the third and fourth inning, I dropped the rosin bag and pine tar onto the on-deck circle. On my way back to the dugout, I saw Ricky jogging out wearing an Angels' uniform.

"Van, you're wanted in the clubhouse," he said.

"What's up, why are you wearing a uniform?"

"Don't worry about it. I'm taking over for you, just get inside."

"Sure, I'll go in after this inning."

"No, Van, you have to go in now."

I jogged down the steps and through the tunnel connecting the dugout to the clubhouse. *What was so important*? *What did I do*? I hoped that I was not in trouble. I swung open the clubhouse door. Greg stood at the entrance—minus his usual grumpy look.

"Van, come with me," he said.

"What did I do? The wings couldn't have been *that* hot."

"Wings? No, Van, this has nothing to do with wings," Greg said, leading me through the hallway. He opened the door and suddenly, nothing made sense.

CHAPTER
9

"Mom?"

"Van," she cried as she wrapped her arms around me. She was shaking, nearly convulsing.

"Mom, what's going on?"

"Van, Van, Van ..." she repeated between sobs. I felt an unexplained heaviness building deep within my abdomen. Without knowing any of the answers, it worked its way up through my chest. My heart pounded and felt like it was squeezing its way through my carotid artery.

"Mom, what's going on, what's wrong, where's Dad?" My eyes blurred. The pounding in my head and chest muffled the sounds of traffic and people.

"Accident ..." was the only word she got out before she broke down again, still clinging to me as if I were trying to escape. Greg standing behind her, caught my eye and said, "Van, your dad was in a very bad accident."

It felt like my heart found its way into my head, everything slowed down. The answers did not come fast enough. For the first time, I noticed a Washington State Patrol, standing a few feet behind Mom.

"What happened?" I screamed at him. The concourse was swimming and I saw Greg's lips moving, but I didn't hear anything, the words sounded like they were miles away. Blackness took over—the kind that you knew would take up residence for a while.

The officer stepped in. "We've cleared out and arranged for you to move into the player's family lounge, please follow me."

"Mom, is Dad okay?"

"No, Van, he isn't," she barely said as the police officer led us, like victims in a concentration camp. The short walk through the sallow hall felt like an eternity. We entered the lounge and immediately a mortal silence enveloped the room.

"That can't be, he dropped me off this afternoon. No, something's wrong!" I said through a stream of tears. The anger and rage competed with the blackness inside. They had to be wrong, this kind of thing only happened in the movies. My heart shouted in protest, as if by sheer force of will I could fix the devastation that occurred.

Mom made a heroic attempt, cutting through the sobs. "Oh, Van, he was driving home about two hours ago, I had just gotten off the phone with him—something happened …"

The reality coalesced and I lost it. I toppled onto the couch and fell to the floor. The darkness deepened until I was on the precipice of a hideous void. Blackness was everywhere. Black turned to grey as I regained consciousness. Mom bent down and gave me water. I pushed it away and attempted to pull myself onto the sofa. It felt like trying to bench press four hundred pounds. I fell back to the plush carpeting.

"Van, just lay still, don't move," I barely heard her say. My senses returned to me. My heart felt like it moved back into the right position, but the blackness lurked just beneath the surface.

"Someone, tell me what happened," I pleaded.

The officer stepped forward. "We are still investigating the details. Your father was involved in a single car collision. An eyewitness phoned 911. The paramedics performed CPR without success. They pronounced him dead at the scene. I'm sorry, son. They did all they could."

I sat up slowly and looked at Mom. I will never forget the look in her eyes at that moment. Our rock, the foundation of our family, had been ripped away from us. The blackness inside me receded a bit when I realized that she needed me right now. Reaching for her, I smelled the hours of tears that saturated her clothes. I held her and didn't say a word as she continued to cry. My eyes were swollen and my head felt like it was being squeezed by a vice grip, however the darkness continued to recede.

Dad is gone, I thought. I remembered how just hours ago we were tossing the ball. He was the happiest I had seen him in years. Listening to him talk about working from home and starting his own business, it was as if he had finally found his passion. He was full of life that was now gone. Deep in my soul, a light went out.

A catalyst initiated a reaction that grew from the smallest reaches of my soul. "Don't worry, Mom, we're going to get through this, we're a team." I looked up to the officer. "What do we need to do now? What do you need from us?"

"When you're ready, I would like to take you to the morgue so that you can collect his things and have a moment alone," he replied.

"Van, anything you need, let me know," Greg offered as he wiped away his own tears.

CHAPTER
10

The next few days were a blur. Mom and I worked through our new life together the best we could. We broke down at the strangest times, during a commercial for Disneyland, picking up the paper in the morning, at night while trying to eat. Night was the hardest. It seemed especially lonely the first few nights. We didn't get much sleep and found ourselves attacking peanut butter, pretzels or ice cream at about two in the morning

Zoe and Fred were great. They came over after school every day to help and to keep us company. Fred went from manager back to being a best friend. Mom and Dad's friends and family would stop in at random times—dropping off food, attempting conversation or would just sit and stare blankly at the walls. There wasn't much to say.

In the background, Mom played the usual parade of talking heads on the television. It was the same every day with Chris Matthews, Lawrence O'Donnell, Ed Schultz and *The Rachel Maddow Show*. I never understood what my parents saw in all of that, but they both loved to watch and talk about those shows. I suppose that was her way to cope. I remembered how Mom would have it on during the day, and then Dad would join in on the replays at night. I asked Mom once a while back, "How can you watch that stuff twice?" She responded saying, "I don't absorb these things the way your dad does, and sometimes it takes me a couple of times to get what's really happening."

With the Mariners on the road, school offered a distraction. It felt like the whole student population knew about what had happened. The school offered the services of grief counseling to help me during this time. The truth was, and I know that I was probably in denial, I felt like I was experiencing a real transformation. With Dad gone, I wanted to help more at home and be there for Mom. They met as high school sweethearts and had been together ever since. She had never worked a paying job while married to him, although, she was very involved with the PTA during elementary school and with volunteering at the hospital. I was always impressed by how she put others first.

On Wednesday, she walked in after a meeting at Biotrust and plopped down on the dining room chair. "Well, Van, do you want to know the good news or the bad news first?"

"Let's start with the good news. We can both use some of that," I replied.

"It looks like your dad set us up pretty good. Biotrust just informed me that your father had a million dollar life insurance policy that the company had taken out for him. Combine that with the $500,000 policy that we had together, we should be in pretty good shape financially."

"And the bad news?"

"He's still gone..." Mom said as she broke down crying again. I couldn't contain it either, I tried to hold back the tears, swallowing lumps in my throat, looking outside at the beautiful spring day, anything to avoid crying again. Inevitably, the tide returned as if being pulled by a full moon and the tears flowed. Sometimes, at moments like this, I felt like we would never get over the loss and despair. After a few minutes, I said, "Let's go for a walk. We need to get outside for a while and see where our feet lead us."

It was beautiful outside, finally warming up after a long, grey winter. The spring flowers were in bloom and for the first time, I realized what "hope springs eternal" really meant. We walked over to the neighborhood playground and jumped on the swings. The feeling of the back and forth with the little stomach jumps at the top of the arc, helped to ease the reality of our situation.

On our way back, we passed a home with a black Labrador retriever puppy frolicking in the front yard with a couple of kids. The dog bounded up to us—I bent down to pet him and got a face full of pink dog tongue. Mom cracked up and I realized that it was the first time that I had watched her laugh in a long time. Bending down, Mom looked to get some of her own kisses from the dog. I stood back, watching as an idea formed. One of my friends at school had a litter of lab puppies. It was the perfect thing for Mom.

After we returned home, we dove into the food left by family and friends. We laughed and talked about nothing, silly things to pass the time and get through another day. Shooing Mom out of the kitchen, I volunteered to clean up. When finished, I passed the family room and there she was, with her new best friend, *The Rachel Maddow Show*. I stopped and watched for a minute. Rachel was hosting something called Geek Week, and her guest from MIT was talking about new technology that could potentially levitate objects. I wasn't sure if it was a joke or not, but Mom seemed entertained.

"Good night, Mom, I love you," I said while giving her a big hug. I retreated to my room, and closed the door.

This was the worst time. I looked around and everything reminded me of Dad. The pictures, the certificate of accomplishment from the Biotrust open house, the model rockets that we loved to shoot together. I picked up the Berg card from the nightstand. I sat, staring at it. This ordinary card offered so much more meaning now.

I pulled out the holder that I had found in Thompson's locker and popped Moe Berg into it. Of course, it was a perfect fit. I set it on my nightstand and left to brush my teeth. I was tired tonight. It had been a long week and was going to get longer. Friday night would be the memorial service where we would say goodbye to Dad for the last time. *Goodbye to Dad*. The statement felt so foreign, so unnatural.

Climbing into bed, I reached over and turned the light off. Pulling my arm back, I knocked the baseball card holder, with Moe Berg going along for the ride, onto the floor. I leaned over the bed and grabbed the holder. Moe had popped out. Picking it up, it felt warm. *How could that be, maybe from the lamp*? I thought. I checked the holder and it was cool. I clicked on the lamp and investigated the card a little closer. It looked like a normal card. I was too tired to care and decided to leave the phenomenon for another time.

CHAPTER
11

Mom was still sleeping while I hurried off to school. Fred and Zoe were waiting for me when I arrived. They had become my support group and had taken it upon themselves to be there for me as often as possible.

"Hi, Van," they said in unison and then gave each other a stupid look.

"Hey, guys, have you seen Veronica around?" I asked.

Zoe scrunched her face ever so slightly. "No, why?"

"I heard she had some lab puppies and I wanted to get one for my mom. I think she would love a puppy and it would be a great distraction."

"She's in my second period," offered Fred. "You want me to tell her you're looking for her?"

"That'd be great. I really hope she still has one. You should have seen my mom light up when we were playing with a dog on our walk yesterday."

"What a great idea. Have you ever had a dog before?" Zoe asked.

"No, but how hard could it be? Besides, it would give her a break from everything that's happening."

We decided to meet after second period. When I walked up, Fred, Zoe and Veronica were waiting at the locker. I took that as a good sign.

"As it turns out, I have one puppy left and would love for you to have it," Veronica announced. "We've been charging three hundred dollars, but my mom said you can have him for free. Maybe you can leave me some tickets for a Mariners' game sometime?"

"That's awesome," I said. "Of course you can have some tickets to a game. When can I come over to get him?"

"If you want, you can come over after school today. My mom's so happy that he's for you."

"Thanks, Veronica, I'll come over right after we get out."

"Oh, Van, can I come with you, I would love to see your new pal?" Zoe asked.

"Yeah, sure, of course. Do you think your mom can run us to the pet store before we pick up the pup?"

"I know she has to pick up my brother from my grandparent's house, but I'll check. If not, we have extra collars and leashes. We can give you some food, too."

"Awesome, this is going better than I thought it would."

School crawled by the rest of the day. It felt like a week later when the final bell rang.

When Zoe and I got to her house, the leash and collar were waiting by the front door.

"Pink?"

"Sorry, I forgot to warn you about the color."

"That's okay. He'll be sporting a Mariners' leash before too long."

We arrived at Veronica's house and knocked. The door flew open and a little ball of black fur tumbled out. He was the cutest puppy I had ever seen. The compact lump of energy couldn't walk straight and kept falling over his already huge paws. He came right to me and licked me with a tongue that was half sandpaper and half slime.

"Veronica, he's perfect—my mom's gonna love him. Just let me know when your family wants to come to a game. Thanks so much, I can't wait to get him home."

Zoe left me when we passed her house and I ran the rest of the way home. Turning the corner to the house, I saw Mom's car in the driveway. Trying to think of a clever way to give her our new puppy, I decided the direct approach would be best.

"MOM, MOM, YOU HAVE TO COME OUT HERE, QUICK!" I screamed.

"Van, what's wrong, what happened?" she shouted from inside the house with a sound of terror in her voice. Maybe this approach wasn't such a good idea after all. The door flew open, banging against the house so hard the hinges wobbled. Bolting onto the porch, she skidded to a stop.

"Van, what is—" suddenly she went silent. With one look at the new addition to our family, she burst into tears and laughed at the same time. "Oh, Van! I can't believe you did this. He is adorable! Or is it a she?" She pulled the critter out of my arms and wrapped him up in hers. The black half-pint of fur smothered her in kisses.

"It's a boy. So, what do you think, can we keep him?"

"Van Stone, are you crazy?" she asked. "Of course we can keep him. What should we name him?"

"That's up to you, Mom."

"How about Jake?" Mom offered in about two point five nanoseconds.

"That's perfect, he looks like a Jake. Let's take him in for food and water." With that, our family was back to three. Jake would never fill the shoes that were missing, but at least he was a distraction, for now. Over time, he would help alleviate the aching in our hearts.

Throughout the rest of the night, we dog proofed our home. We rolled around on the floor with our new friend, laughing until we cried. After about three hours, Jake's tongue dragged on the ground. We gave him a bowl of milk and Mom took him to his new bed, in her room.

We realized we were tired too, and decided to call it a night. Tomorrow was going to be a long day. I straggled to my room, dreading the finality that lay ahead.

In the quiet of the night, a muffled crash came from somewhere in the house.

"What was that?" I whispered aloud. I listened intently and heard nothing else. Creeping out of my room, I tiptoed across the hall and cracked open Mom's door. The sliver of light from the hallway illuminated the tipped over puppy box. Opening the door further, I saw little Jake's head sticking out from under the covers and Mom with a contented look on her face. Both fast asleep.

CHAPTER
12

Friday arrived early with the yelping of our new puppy. I raced out of my room to find Mom, eyes half-open, holding Jake.

"Here, he's yours. I don't think I slept at all last night."

"Aw, come on, Mom, it couldn't have been that bad?" I asked.

"No, it wasn't—I'm just tired, I guess. Do you mind if I rest a little while longer, before you leave for school?"

"Go ahead, I'll give Jake some food and take him outside."

I raced down the stairs and bounced out the front door. I lowered Jake and he immediately fell over his big feet. I sat on the stoop and watched him as he explored the great outdoors. It was a warm, almost summer morning. The sun was already shining, which was unusual this time of the year, when it normally took until noon for the fog to burn off.

I watched a garbage truck working its way down the street. As it pulled away from our neighbor's house, diagonally across the street, I noticed a nondescript black sedan parked along the curb.

"I've never seen that car here before, Jake. Let's go check it out." I scooped him up and started out to the sidewalk. Instantly, the car backed up and jetted out of the parking spot, overtaking the garbage truck in about three seconds. "Whoa, did you see that, Jake?" I ran into the road, only to see a cloud of dust settling at the next corner.

Jake didn't take much notice. He was more interested in licking my face. "I'm sure it's nothing," I said to Jake. We went up to my room to get ready for school.

Back in my room, I spotted the Berg card on the night table. Remembering the phenomenon from two nights ago, I picked up the card, placed it in the holder and threw it on the bed while I got dressed. After about five minutes, I tested it. The card had heated up again. I replaced it with a Cantos card. Nothing. It didn't heat up at all.

"This is getting very strange," I said to Jake. He didn't really care. He was chewing on my shoe and loving every moment of it. "Jake, stop it," I shouted. He stumbled over to me as I slid to the floor from the bed. Jake sniffed the holder and made a quiet whining noise.

"Don't worry, buddy—it's nothing." Checking the Berg card, I noticed that it had cooled off. It was late, so I tossed the holder and card into my backpack and grabbed a few more cards to check out later.

I took Jake back to Mom's room. "He's all yours, I've gotta run."

"Thanks for the little extra time this morning. You are truly my hero."

"No problem, Mom. Is it okay if Zoe and Fred come home with me after school?"

"Of course, you're a lucky kid to have friends like them," Mom said.

"I sure am. Bye, Mom," I said as I took a step toward the door and stopped. Reversing direction, I walked to the bed, gave Mom a big hug and said, "I love you, Mom."

A Cliff Bar made for a perfect breakfast as I grabbed it on the way out and headed to school.

Today didn't feel the same as other Fridays, the day dragged. There was a cloud of seriousness that had settled in. I wasn't looking forward to tonight. It seemed as if Dad would come back as long as we didn't do anything official to say goodbye. There was no way to avoid the finality that tonight would bring.

During lunch, I met up with Fred. Sitting at the table, I rifled through my backpack.

"Aren't you going to eat?" Fred asked.

"Nah, I'm not very hungry today. Hey, Fred, check this out. I found this baseball card holder in Mark Thompson's locker after the first series. At first, I didn't think much about it, I thought it might be some new promo thing from the card companies, but check this out." I snapped the Moe Berg Card in the right side compartment and after about a minute, it heated up.

Fred grabbed it and turned it in every direction. "Maybe it's a hologram projection thing, like in *Star Wars*. Where's the on-off switch?"

"That's the thing, there isn't one. Now, take out the Berg card and put in any one of these." I handed him a stack and he pulled the warmed Berg card out and put in Eric Cooper's card.

"So, what am I waiting for? It's not doing anything."

"Now, put the Berg card in the left side," I said.

Fred did as instructed. "It's still not doing anything."

"That's right. The Berg card only warms up when it's on the right side. That's the mystery—why *only* the Berg card and why *only* on the right side? My dad gave me the card right before the season started, as a gift. I just found this holder a couple of days ago. I've tried tons of other cards and nothing happens."

"I don't know, Van, maybe the card is …" Fred sang the *Twilight Zone* music, "… radioactive."

"Hey, do you think?" I asked.

"No, dude, I'm just kidding—what's up with you, it's just a baseball card."

"I think I'm going to go ask Mr. Han to check it out, he has a Geiger counter." I grabbed my stuff and hurried out of the lunchroom.

Mr. Han was the resident teacher freak. He was a great science teacher, but most people think that he had one too many Bunsen burner accidents. He owned a Geiger counter because he was constantly trying to prove that the Hanford nuclear power plant and disposal site had leaked over to Western Washington. His theory, which he told every chance he had, was that the radioactive waste from the largest nuclear waste dump in the country, would infiltrate our water supply and we would contract radiation poisoning. Opening the door, I interrupted him trying to get a reading from a turkey sandwich that he was about to eat.

"Hi, Mr. Han!"

"Oh—hi, Van, just checking out my lunch. Looks okay, but I know it's coming sooner or later. What can I do for you?"

"You have just what I need. Could you check out something with your Geiger counter?"

"What? Yes! Finally—some real radiation! What is it, Van. *Where* is it—do you have it in a lead box? Wait—you were exposed? I should get my lead blanket, no sense in both of us going down!"

"I wasn't exposed to anything. It's nothing like that," I said as I pulled out my mystery holder. "It's this contraption—a baseball card holder. It looks pretty normal, but when ..."

"They all look normal!" He screamed as he cut me off and then ripped it out of my hands.

"I think you should try and settle down, Mr. Han. As I was explaining, when I put any random baseball card into it, nothing happens. But, when I put this card," I held up the Berg card for him to see, "in the right side, it starts to warm up. Check it out."

"Hmm, that's interesting, Van. What happens next, does it keep getting hotter?" he asked excitedly.

"No, that's it. It warms up and nothing happens. It doesn't get any hotter and nothing happens when I put it in the left side."

"Oh, that's disappointing, but strange indeed. Let's let our inquisitive Geiger counter take a look." With that, he held the instrument near the holder containing the card and flipped the dial. The needle jumped up and settled back down to zero. He moved the wand all around, but the needle wouldn't budge. With a disillusioned look on his face he said, "Whatever you have here, it's not radioactive."

"That's good news."

"For you maybe, but I know I'll find some eventually. They're coming to get us!" he said.

"Who's coming to get us?"

"Did I say 'they', oh, I meant the Hanford waste is going to get into our water supply. Yeah, that's what I meant," he said and stared out the window.

"Uh … yeah, sure, whatever you say. Thanks for checking it out, Mr. Han." I turned and headed out as the school bell prompted me to move on to my next class.

The school day finally crawled to and end. Zoe and Fred waited for me outside. The sun was shining with a slight marine breeze, the kind of day that should make you happy. I guess some things couldn't conquer a mood. Walking home, we kept quiet. Fred was unusually solemn, like he was afraid to be himself.

Zoe broke the tension and asked, "Fred keeps telling me about an alien device you found in someone's locker at the clubhouse. What's he talking about?"

"So, what did Mr. Han say, am I right?" Fred was about to bust and jumped in front of the two of us. I knew he couldn't keep mellow for long. "It's radioactive, isn't it? I started to think more about it and what I think …"

"Fred! Chill out, what is wrong with you," I said, not letting him continue, "there's nothing to it. Mr. Han looked at it and tested it. Nothing." I pushed him out of the way and continued walking. Realizing that I had snapped at Fred, I felt bad, "Sorry, let's just keep going."

"What's going on?" Zoe asked. "He couldn't possibly have been telling me the truth, right?"

"No, as usual, Fred's trying to make something out of nothing. I found a baseball card holder. It's no big deal. I really appreciate you guys coming with me, but do you mind if we just walk. I really don't feel like trying to solve any mysteries right now." The gravity of the tonight's event pressed down on me as we moved closer to the house.

As we arrived, the street in front of the house looked like a used car lot. I took a deep breath. *Here we go*, I thought.

Inside, I noticed an aunt and uncle from Olympia. I remembered he did something in politics. I was surprised I hadn't seen him on any of the shows Mom and Dad watched. *Whoops, there I go again.*

A few of Mom's close friends gave me hugs and told me how sorry they were. That was something that I couldn't understand. They all said, "We're so sorry for your loss." It wasn't as if I lost a game in the ninth inning by giving up a grand slam. My dad was gone. Couldn't they think of something better to say than, "I'm sorry for your loss"? A few more people that I didn't recognize approached and gave me hugs.

The place started smelling like old women's perfume. My chest started tightening, so I turned and began walking toward the door. I caught fragments of sentences within the whispers.

"He's too young to lose his father."

"Poor thing, I can't even imagine."

"I wonder how he's handling this."

Don't they realize that I lost my dad, not my hearing? I threw open the front door and the warm afternoon heated my face. I plopped down on the stoop. Zoe and Fred followed me outside and sat on either side of me. They each put an arm around my shoulders. I looked toward Fred and watched him stare into space. Turning to Zoe, I saw tears trickling down her cheek. The three of us sat—not saying a word.

I heard the door open and Mom dropped a black blob on the porch. "Go say hi, Jake."

Jake lumbered up to my back and pushed his nose between Zoe and me. The three of us watched as Jake started climbing onto my lap. Halfway up, he rolled down the couple of steps, landing on his back. A quick squirm returned him to upright and he bounced back toward me.

"He's great, Van," Fred said. "You didn't tell me he was so cute. Let me hold him. Come here, little guy." I handed him over as I looked up to Mom, who was doing her best to pull off a smile.

"Thanks, Mom," I said.

"How are you doing, Van?" she asked.

"Well, I was feeling kind of smothered in there. Otherwise, I'm okay, I guess. When do we need to leave for the service?"

"In about ten minutes," she responded sadly. "Why don't you let Jake run around a bit and make sure he does his 'business' and then we can get going."

CHAPTER
13

I thought there were a lot of people at my house, but that was nothing compared to the number of people at the memorial service. The place was packed. We followed Mom into the common area. A man dressed formally walked up to me and offered his condolences. Mom must have already met him because he didn't express any condolences to her. I introduced my friends and he led us into the main room.

Large drapes decorated the dimly lit room and hung half-open over the windows. The plush carpeting dampened any sound that anyone dare make. We worked our way toward the front of the room and the crowd parted, as if it were the

Red Sea. That was when I saw it—the closed mahogany casket sitting in front of the room, on display. There were huge flower bouquets everywhere and pictures of Dad from when he was a young kid, until just a few weeks ago at a Mariners' game.

Mom lost it. I followed right behind. Zoe hesitated as she tried to hold back the tears. Fred took off. We were ushered to a row of chairs and as I sat down, the full weight of the circumstances rushed back at me. There was no escaping it now—no dogs to play with, school to attend or baseball card holders to make up some wild story about. This was the real deal.

The seemingly endless line of mourners approached, one by one, offering more apologies, as if they were the ones responsible. As the minutes ticked off the clock, I sat there holding Mom's hand, wishing we could be with Dad again. The weight of the loss was too much. I closed my eyes, willing myself to think of anywhere but here.

When I opened my eyes, I realized that Zoe had slipped away a while ago. I felt a sudden need for Fred's goofiness and Zoe's compassion. Scanning the room, I didn't see them, and then my eyes made contact with Mom. Without saying a word, she nodded her head and gave a little quick tilt to the left.

"Are you sure?" I asked.

"I'll be fine. You could use a little break."

"Alright, I won't be gone long. I'll just get a breath of fresh air and stretch my legs." She barely heard what I said as an old friend from California approached her, arms outstretched.

I found Zoe and Fred hanging outside with the last rays of daylight. The sky was perfectly clear with a deep blue, almost purple look. To the west, an orange glow provided a backdrop for the silhouette of the Olympic Mountains.

Chasing the sun on the horizon, a blue-white Venus blazed in the dusk.

"Hey, guys, I bet you've had enough," I said.

"Nah, we're just out here getting some fresh air. It's rather crowded in there with all of those people. Your dad must have known half of Seattle," Fred said.

"I can't believe it either," I added. "I don't even know a quarter of these people. My mom said that most of them came from his work. Zoe, thanks for hanging in there with me for as long as you did."

"I just wanted to be there if you needed anything. Not like Fred who took off because he didn't want you to see him cry."

"What! You didn't see me crying," Fred exclaimed.

"Oh—so you must have been dripped on by the air conditioning vent," Zoe said as she punched him on the arm. "When you and your mom got busy with the family, I figured it would be a great time to slip away and see if Fred needed me out here."

"I don't need anything, I already told you. I don't like crowds," Fred insisted. "Besides, my parents are on their way and I wanted to call them and make sure they didn't get lost."

"Um, what's that thing on their dashboard—a G-P-S?" Zoe teased.

"Give me a break, huh?" Fred pleaded.

"Hey, Van." I spun around as Ricky walked up with Greg.

"I can't believe you guys are here. You didn't have to do this," I said.

"Don't worry about it. We consider you one of us, a part of the family," Ricky said.

"How're you doing, Van?" Greg asked. "Is your mom doing okay? I know this must be really tough for the both of you."

He seemed like a completely different person. I couldn't believe that he was here. "We're hanging in there ... there's not much else we can do," I said. *At least he didn't say "I'm sorry for your loss"*, I thought.

"Well, like I told you before, if there is anything I can do, let me know. Take as much time off as you need. Ricky can cover for you."

"Thanks, but I really need to get back. It'll help me take my mind off what's happened. Hey, guys, this is Greg, my boss, and Ricky, the clubbie that works with me."

"Hey, I'm your boss too, don't forget," Ricky said.

"Yeah, Yeah, I know. Actually, he's been showing me the ropes. Anyway, these are my best friends, Zoe and Fred."

"Nice to meet you guys, when you come to the ballpark, make sure to come by and say hi," Ricky said.

"Ricky, you're supposed to be working, not fraternizing with the fans," Greg lectured. He turned to me and said, "We're going in to see your mom, we'll look for you on our way out." They walked away as Greg continued to lay into Ricky, both of their hands flying in the air as they each made their point.

"Is that guy always like that?" Fred asked.

"He's pretty gruff most of the time, but the day it happened he was like a different person. He definitely has a good side to him. One thing for sure—he's a straight shooter. With him, you always know where you stand." I looked back to the growing volume of mourners. "I should get back inside. What do you think?"

"No problem, Van, I'll go with you." Zoe grabbed my arm and turned toward the door.

"Hey, I'll go, too. Wait up," Fred said.

We waded through the throngs and then veered off to the perimeter where there were less people. Feigned smiles were everywhere, the kind that people do when they don't know you or have no idea what else to do. A couple of mourners stopped me to offer their condolences. With each one, I sensed Fred getting more and more uncomfortable. We broke off from one of the many contrived conversations and made a dash for an opening in the masses. The three of us huddled together, as if we were mapping out our next play, so that no other mourners would come up to us.

I peered over Zoe—and froze.

CHAPTER
14

"**F**red—don't look now, but remember those creepy Suits I told you about, from the ballpark? They're standing over in the corner," I whispered.

Of course, Fred immediately whipped his head around in their direction. They stood next to some flowers, wearing the suits and sunglasses, looking like they were trying to blend in with the crowd.

"I said *don't* look!" I said in my loudest whisper. "Now they know we saw them."

"Come on, Van, they can't be hiding, they're in plain sight. What's the big deal? I'm going to go over there and find out who they are," Fred said as he broke from our huddle.

Instantly, the Suits turned together and bolted through an emergency exit. Fred picked up his pace and headed for the same door. *Oh jeez*, I thought. *Here we go.* I grabbed Zoe and we worked our way through the crowd, toward the main entrance. Feeling like salmon swimming against the current, we finally reached the main door, and jogged out into the dark. Fred was shaking his fist in the air and screaming, as a black sedan chirped its tires and pulled out of the parking lot.

"Fred, what happened?"

"By the time I got out of the room, they were almost in their car. I ran out, screaming at them to stop. They just ignored me and when they opened their doors, they stopped for a second. They looked straight at me, as if they were ID'ing me. I'm sure they logged me into their memory banks. Then they jumped in and you saw the rest. It's weird, they move way too smoothly. Something's up."

"Did you get a license number?" Zoe asked.

"Yeah, I think I saw a nine."

"A *nine*—you think you saw a *NINE*? Zoe fumed. "What is that—a joke?"

"What?" Fred said defensively. "I'm just telling you what I thought I saw. Besides, it was getting dark and they bolted way too fast."

"Whatever—guys, this is the third or fourth time I've seen them. I think they were even on my street the other day when I took Jake out," I said.

"Why would they take off like that?" Zoe asked.

"What's up with those guys, do you think they're following you?" Fred asked.

"I don't know. Why would anyone want to follow me?"

"You're right, there's not much reason to follow you, unless—do you think they're paparazzi? I didn't see any cameras," Fred said disappointedly.

"Sometimes you are so lame," I said, "but this is no longer a coincidence. I should ask my mom if she's seen them."

We walked back in. Nobody had noticed the minicommotion. I caught a glimpse of Zoe's parents talking with my mom. The crowd had thinned out a little. A louder murmur of voices replaced the previous hush in the room.

I spotted Greg and Ricky talking in the corner. They looked like two people who were deciding if they had stood around long enough and if it was okay to leave. Locking on to us, they moved through the crowd, zeroing in on the only people they knew.

Greg reached into his back pocket and pulled out a card. "Van, I forgot to give this to you earlier. It came to you, addressed to the clubhouse."

Taking the envelope, I wondered, *who would send me something at the clubhouse?* The return address was a post office box in Oakland, no name. I ripped it open and pulled out a condolence card.

Van,

I'm really sorry about your dad. I heard about it through one of my buddies on the Angels. It is a tough thing to lose your father at such a young age. I know how it is, because I lost my dad when I was 13. If there is anything I can do for you, please let me know.

Your Friend,
Ron Cantos

My face flushed. A cross between being embarrassed, because it was cool to get something personal from such a star, and realizing I shouldn't be feeling this way.

"What is it, Van?" asked Fred.

"Yeah, Van, what's wrong, you're turning red?" Zoe chimed in.

"It's a card from Ron Cantos," I replied.

"*What*? That guy is awesome," Fred said. "I can't believe he sent you a card."

"Dude, I thought that guy hated you. He was giving you crap the whole series," Ricky said.

"I know, but by the end of the series he was being really nice to me. I don't know why, but he was. I guess I read him wrong from the beginning."

Mom walked up to our little gathering. "Van, you should mingle around a little more. Most people are getting ready to leave. I know a lot of our friends and family want to say goodbye."

"Sure, Mom, but look at this, I got a card from one of the ballplayers." I handed her the card.

"That's very nice of him. I didn't realize that you got to know any of the players that well. Let's go say goodbye to your aunt and uncle, they're waiting for us." As she led me away, I turned and shrugged my shoulders to my group of friends.

"Don't worry, Van," Greg offered. "I'll see you next week, and you can come in whenever you're ready."

"Bye, Van," Ricky said.

"Thanks for coming, I'll see you guys on Monday," I insisted.

We made our rounds saying goodbye to the mourners. I looked toward the door and saw Zoe and Fred—they had stayed until the bitter end.

"Mrs. Stone, can we help carry some things to the car?" Fred asked.

"That would be nice. Thanks, Fred," she replied. "Don't keep your parents waiting too long, though."

"It's no problem. They're outside talking with Zoe's parents."

We packed up some of the smaller flowers and pictures, and we said our goodbyes. Zoe and Fred carried the boxes out to the car, leaving Mom and I alone. The room was finally empty. Silence. What a strange sensation, it was so quiet that I heard a ringing in my ears. Arm in arm, we worked our way toward the casket. Instinctively, we both put our free hand out and touched the polished wood. This was the last time that I would ever feel his physical presence, even if it were just in the shape of a box.

We said nothing. There were no more tears. The well had gone dry— for now.

"Goodbye, Dad."

"Goodbye, Jack."

We strolled out as the formal man turned off the lights. Walking out into the cool evening, we stepped onto the empty parking lot. Gravel crunched under our feet as a chorus of frogs serenaded us. Bright stars pierced the blackness on this clear night. Looking up, the universe felt larger than ever. I realized it was because our family took up less space in this world with just two of us. Dad was gone forever.

CHAPTER
15

Mom and I worked on our new life as the next few months dragged on. She spent a lot of time getting the finances organized and dealing with insurance companies. With her increased hours volunteering at the hospital, she worked almost as much as a full-time employee. In the evenings, she sat and told me about her favorite things, like transporting patients from their rooms to X-ray or nuclear medicine. Listening to her, I felt the sense of fulfillment she received from talking to the patients, helping make their day a little brighter.

Fred continued to act as my agent and ticket broker. He was amazing. The guy had people lining up for tickets and was getting plenty of extra lunches and other perks at my expense. I didn't really care, though. He was having fun and not hurting anyone.

Zoe was awesome. She continued to surprise me by always being there when I needed someone for support. I think that Mom liked having her and Fred over to the house. It made things full of life and laughter.

As for me, the car issue had been resolved. Mom decided that with our new situation, an extra mode of transportation was indeed necessary. We picked up a used Volvo. Safety was her biggest concern, and I had to admit that I didn't blame her, even if I didn't own the coolest looking car in town.

It was tough without Dad. Occasionally, I'd catch myself thinking he was going to walk in the door. While Mom and I still had our difficult moments, we tried to keep busy and not let the sad times overcome the good ones. A simple philosophy, but it had gotten us through the last few months.

My time in the clubhouse and on the field had been great. I met ballplayers from good teams and bad, nice guys and jerks, and had fun all the way. I was dumped into a garbage can, made a bunch of tips and had been sent on the classic search for the batter's box key. I couldn't wait for summer break, so that I could spend more time at the ballpark. The dreaded Yankees were coming into town this weekend, but first I had to get through the last day of school.

The entire school was electrified. The seniors were the worst, but I came prepared. Last weekend, I picked up the latest Super Soaker Hydro Cannon. Soggy toilet paper draped the main hall, most of it clinging to the lockers. The students lined the hallway, armed to the teeth. It was like walking through a firing squad, with squirt guns and super soakers discharging from everywhere. I had to have a plan.

Scoping out the first break in the lockers, I saw a gap. I bolted for the opening, while avoiding a group from the football team that was at a forty-five degree angle from me. Three streams of water shot out of their weapons as I slid on my knees, just below their arc. I returned fire and scrambled into the small cleft between the lockers. My reconnaissance revealed my next objective, a tall trash can about twenty feet on the opposite side. Several students ran through the gauntlet, heads down and arms up. They took incoming from all sides, getting completely soaked. The seniors were everywhere—the basketball team to my left, the track team sprinting from side to side, and the chess team at the end of the hall. As expected, they had the superior strategic position.

I saw a rather large sophomore from my English class coming toward me. With a goofy grin, he walked through the volley of water as if it were a summer day. I waited and jumped out into the hallway, using him for cover. I walked backwards, directly in front of him, as the football players drenched him from the rear. Their attention shifted to a new group entering the hallway, so I rotated around my cover, to his backside, as the basketball team unloaded on his front.

Ten more steps—then I dove to the shelter of the trashcan. The sophomore stopped at his locker as the football and basketball players moved in for the kill. I only had a second to determine my next move—I rolled under his outstretched arm and sprinted for the end of the hallway. The chess team opened fire as I ducked behind an open locker. I found Veronica, cowering behind her textbooks. Grabbing her arm, I pulled her behind me to shield her from the enemy fire. Reaching around the locker, I returned fire, realizing my reservoir was getting low. Over the shouts and commotion in the hallway, I heard a high-pitched call for "refill" from the chess champion of the school. That was my chance.

"Later, Veronica, you're on your own now," I said and bolted around the corner, crashing into Zoe and Fred. Zoe's usually flowing hair looked like Samara's from *The Ring*—drenched, tangled and matted to her face. Fred, trying to wring out his shirt, was carrying a small *Toy Story* squirt gun.

"Van, are you crazy? Why are you attacking the seniors?" Fred asked.

"*Attack*? I was protecting myself," I responded, assessing my condition. I had made it through senior hall with hardly a drop of water on me. "Zoe, you look like your blow dryer broke this morning. We should have coordinated our entrance so that I could have defended you guys."

"Yeah, I saw Fred outside and he told me he would protect me with his awesome firepower. What did you call it, Fred, 'Shock and Awe'?"

"Hey, didn't my skills compensate for the size of my weapon?"

"Your *skills*? You pushed me in front of you like a human shield. Remind me not to call you when I need rescuing."

"Listen, the worst part is over," I said. "All we have to do is get through the day, then it's summer. I can't wait! Fred, are you coming to the game tonight?"

"Better believe it. Friday night, schools out—there's no place I'd rather be."

"What about me?" Ms. Wet Head asked. "I want to go too—"

"I guess so." Fred turned to me with raised eyebrows and whispered, "Do you think she's getting the wrong idea?"

"I'm standing right *here*," Zoe said with an elongated "here." She squeezed a quart of water out of her hair. "I'd rather die a bitter old maid than be with you."

"What?" Fred exclaimed with a look of shock. "I'm so hurt."

"Yeah, right, sure you are. Sometimes I think your eyeballs are going to fall out from staring at girls so much."

"Hey, it's almost summertime and the scenery *is* improving," Fred said with a smile.

"What a pig. I can't believe I'm going to the game with you again."

"You don't have to."

"Admit it, Fred—we're your only real friends. If I didn't go with you, you would be going by yourself."

"That's not true. I could have a ton of people go with me."

"Name one."

I came to Fred's rescue. "Okay, okay. Let's get to class before the chess team gets back."

"Hey, Van, can you get me some seeds and gum tonight?"

"Oh, brother ..." Zoe said quietly.

We made it through the rest of the day without getting soaked. At the final bell, the students went crazy and I got out of there as quickly as possible. Now, I was officially a junior.

CHAPTER
16

The summer heated up uncharacteristically. Temperatures soared into the eighties and nineties. The three of us spent time on Alki Point while the ballclub was on the road. The weeks marched on and for the first time in a long while, I thought that life would turn out all right. Mom, Jake and I had settled into our new routines and we even went to Ocean Shores for a few days and enjoyed the surf.

It was the week before the All-Star break and the Athletics were coming back into town. I looked forward to working with them now that I wasn't running around with my head down, trying to stay out of everybody's way.

The equipment truck arrived late on Thursday evening, following the day game with the Angels. As we unloaded the truck, Mark Thompson walked up with a scowl on his face. It wasn't unusual for the trainers or equipment managers to show up during this process to organize supplies, but I had never seen a player show up. Thompson was perfectly dressed in his usual dark suit, and seemed jumpy. He walked through the winding hallway and sat down at the first locker.

"Hi, Mark, can we help you with something?" Greg asked.

"No, just go about your business, I'm fine," he replied.

A creepy feeling infiltrated my veins as the guilt hit me. *Could he be here because of the holder that I found in his locker?* I wondered. *It couldn't be, that was almost two months ago.* If it were anything important, we would have heard about it. A pitcher for the Red Sox left a lucky rabbit's foot in his locker and he made us FedEx it to him the same day. I was debating whether to say something, when he got up and walked out to the tunnel.

Ricky looked at me. "That guy is seriously weird."

"I know, did you see the way he was acting, the guy needs some Ritalin or something."

"Get back to work you two, no whispering around here, if you have something to say, say it so we can all hear," the paranoid Greg barked. He always thought we were talking about him.

Thompson stood outside the clubhouse door, like a sentry on guard duty, while we unpacked. When the clubhouse was in perfect order, the three of us walked out together. He was gone, just like that. He didn't come back into the clubhouse or say goodbye, just disappeared. Ricky and I laughed about the experience, walking out to our cars.

"Hey, maybe he got demoted and now he's the equipment manager," Ricky snickered.

"Or, maybe he struck out three times today and instead of running laps, they made him come down here," I added.

"Whatever it is, that guy sure has some issues. See ya later, Van," Ricky said climbing into his car.

"He sure does," I agreed. "See you tomorrow."

I slept in and awoke to an empty house, except for a big, black dog sleeping next to my bed. After showering, I dressed and grabbed a stack of baseball cards that included Cantos and threw them in my backpack. Mom was at the hospital volunteering, so I left a note and headed for the ballpark. Driving into the player's parking lot, I looked at all the rides. A Mercedes-Benz S65 that must cost at least $180,000, an Audi R8, a BMW M6 convertible and a Porsche Carrera GT, these ballplayers sure do know how to spend money. I parked my Volvo and walked to the security gate.

The clubhouse was already jamming with music and activity. Cantos dressed at his locker while other teammates played Xbox or cards. He made eye contact and gave a big wave. I waved back and walked toward him.

"Ron, thanks for the card you sent after my dad's accident. That was really nice. I can't believe you even heard about it."

"No problem, Van. The word got out around the team. I'm sorry for you. How've you been doing?"

"It was pretty tough in the beginning, but now it's been getting a little easier. I still miss him like crazy and sometimes I still can't believe that he's gone. Coming to the ballpark sure has helped. Thanks again for thinking of me."

"No prob. My dad was shot and killed when I was thirteen. He was messed up in drugs and gambling, but I didn't know about that stuff. I woke up one morning and he was gone. My mama told me that he was with the angels. After a few weeks of men pounding on our door and asking for money, she picked me up and moved to the west coast. That's when I figured out there was more to the story."

"Wow," was all I could say. Hearing a story like that for the first time, my face gave away my look of shock.

"But that was a long time ago, don't worry. Hey, did you bring the cards for me to sign?" Cantos asked.

"You remembered? I've got them in my backpack—do you want to do it now?"

"I've got some time before BP, let's do it."

I ran over to my locker, grabbed the stack of cards and my Sharpie pen while looking around for Greg. The coast was clear. Sorting through the cards, I handed him a couple and continued to look for more.

"That's cool. You have a couple of my rookie cards. For your sake and mine, I hope they'll be worth something one day. Let me see what else you got," Cantos said as he grabbed the stack out of my hand.

"It's just a bunch of cards, no biggie," I said.

"Eric Cooper! What are you doing with that chumps' card? Jerry Rhett—has he dumped you in a garbage can? He does that to all the rookie batboys."

"Oh, yeah, he got me good last month," I said.

"What's this, Moe Berg? I haven't heard that name before," he said as he flipped the card over. After reading the stats, he asked, "Where did you get it from? Is it worth anything? Whoa, this guy played back in the 1920's, what's up with that?"

"Nah, it's not worth anything, it's a reproduction. My dad gave it to me."

"Your dad gave it to you? Hmm, that's cool. Well, here's the rest of mine, now you have five Ron Cantos cards autographed by the man himself." He handed them back, stood and started toward the clubhouse door.

"Thanks, Ron, I really appreciate it. Let me know if I can do anything for you while you're in town," I said as Thompson sat at his locker, next to where I was standing.

"Hey, batboy, got a second?" Thompson commanded more than asked. He still had his full black suit on. Most guys took off their suit jacket or sport coat as soon as they walked in the door. This team didn't have a dress code, so most of the players didn't even wear suits.

"Sure, what do you need?" I asked.

"Can you get me another pair of sani's, these have a hole in them," he said.

"Uh, sorry about that, we must have missed them." After retrieving a brand new pair out of the bag, I walked back to Thompson's locker and handed him the socks. "Here you go and I'll make sure it won't happen again."

"Thank you. Can I ask you something?"

"Sure."

"What was Cantos talking to you about?"

It's none of your business, I thought, but said, "He was just signing some baseball cards for me."

"Can I see them?" he asked.

"What?" I asked, surprised by his question. I didn't know what to say. "You want to see my baseball cards?"

"If you don't mind, yes, I do," Thompson said.

Handing them over, I said, "I know that we're not supposed to ask for autographs, but the last time he was in town, he told me to bring my cards in so that he could sign them."

Thompson silently studied the cards.

"I never asked him," I said defensively. *Who is this guy, the autograph police*? I thought, and watched as he thumbed through the rest of the cards. He stopped at Moe Berg.

"Where did you get this one?" he snapped.

"My dad gave it to me. What's the big deal anyway? Why does everyone keep asking about it?"

"Who else asked you about it?"

This is getting old, I thought. "If it really matters, Cantos asked me about it. I don't get it, the card isn't worth anything."

"If I were you, I would be careful with him," he said. His face looked tight and his eyes darted around the room, probably to see if Cantos had heard him. Ron was out on the field already, which was where Thompson should be.

"Uh, sure, whatever you say," I replied.

He handed the cards back and turned around without another word. He left me standing, staring at his back. Without any options, I slinked back to my locker.

Ricky was sitting at his adjacent locker. "What was that all about? You're going to get into big trouble with Greg if he catches you pissing off the ballplayers. You know the rules."

"I know! It wasn't me! He called me over and went off on me for no reason. He even told me to be careful with Cantos. Can you believe that? If I was going to watch out for someone it would be that creepy guy."

"I'm just telling you, be careful. Greg is on the warpath today."

I finished dressing and jogged to the field with some extra seeds and gum in my pocket. Sure enough, they were already here. Fred was hanging over the railing trying to talk to the ball girl. Zoe saw me, and a big smile spread across her face.

"Hi, Van, what kind of trouble are you getting into today?" she asked.

"How did you know?"

"Dude, you're getting into trouble? What'd you do?" Fred asked, after his failed attempt to woo the ball girl.

"I didn't get into trouble. That Thompson guy kind of went off on me. I didn't do anything. I don't know—he's just weird."

"Maybe he's on to you about the card holder thing," Fred suggested. "Hey, by the way, do you know that ball girl? Maybe you can hook me up. You can tell her how pimpin' I am."

One-track mind, this guy. "Yeah, I know her, but I wouldn't start that ball rolling if my life depended on it. I have to work with her every day," I said. "Thompson hasn't even mentioned the card holder. He probably never even gave it another thought. Do you realize how much stuff kids send to the players? I just think he's in a bad mood because he's hitting right around the Mendoza line. He might not stay up with the big league club for much longer if he doesn't produce. Honestly, I don't know why he's not in the minors."

"You guys can talk baseball. I'm going to go get a soda. Do you want anything, Fred?" Zoe asked before she headed up the aisle.

"No, thanks, I'm good. I'll just have a sip of whatever you get."

"Your mouth is not going to get *anywhere* near *anything* of mine," Zoe said. "I'll grab a soda for you too." We both watched for a second as she walked up the stairs. Fred gave me a weird look.

"What?" I asked, throwing my hands into the air.

"Um, nothing. Hey, did you score us some seeds?" Fred asked.

"Wow, all you think about is girls and food," I said as I tossed the seeds to Fred.

"Come on, do you blame me?"

Fred and I talked for a while. The crowd filled in. A couple of kids came down for an autograph and I sent them away disappointed. The roof was open on this beautiful summer night. A couple of seagulls swooped down from the top of the stadium and a batted ball sent them scattering.

I looked up and saw Zoe coming back down the aisle with a concerned look on her face.

"Van, I saw the Suits, the ones from the memorial service. They were standing at the top of the aisle, in the concourse. When I walked by, one of them looked at me and gave me a creepy smile. The other one was on the phone and I could have sworn I heard him say—Stone."

"I haven't seen them here for a while. Actually, I haven't seen them since that night. I said something to my mom, but she didn't think it was a big deal. I had forgotten all about them."

"Why did they just say your last name?" Fred asked, trying to create a controversy.

"They were probably just talking about Larry Stone, one of the sports writers for the *Seattle Times*."

"Dude, why do you keep talking like these guys are no big deal?" Fred asked. "With all the times you've seen them don't you think that it's more than just a coincidence? You have to find out who the Suits are. Why don't you just ask Thompson? You know what? Forget it—I'm going up there to find out who they are."

"No, don't do it, Fred!" I shouted. Too late—he was already sprinting up the stairs.

"You know, he's right. You really should find out about those guys, especially after the deal at the funeral home," Zoe said. "Think about it, they keep showing up in strange places and then they take off. If they didn't have anything to hide, why would they run?"

"You're right, but like I said, I haven't seen them in months. Uh-oh, look at Fred," I said pointing toward the concourse. Fred hobbled back down the stairs. His chin had a big red scratch, looking like he had slid into second base with his face.

"What happened?" Zoe and I sang in unison.

"I was running up the steps and just as I was reaching the top, I tripped and did a face-plant on the top step. What a dork. I looked up and the Suits were gone, but I sure got a good laugh out of some fans."

"What a klutz," I said. "Are you okay? They have first aid stations around the concourse, maybe you should go get cleaned up?"

"Nah, I'll just go rinse off in the bathroom."

"Guys, I'll tell you what. Before this series is over, if those two clowns are still around, I'll ask Thompson about them. I'm not looking forward to it, though. He'll probably bite my head off and tell me it's none of my business. I could even lose my job."

"We don't want that to happen. This is my new trolling grounds. I mean, just look around this place," Fred said, looking from side to side.

"How do you put up with him?" I asked Zoe.

"Me? I just ignore him most of the time."

Backing away, I said, "I have to get to work, the team is finishing up infield and I need to change into my gamer. Have fun—and clean up that face of yours."

The rest of the night was uneventful. Oakland lost the game by one run. In the ninth inning, they had a chance with the bases loaded and Thompson up to bat. He promptly hit into a double play to end the game. *I'm no general manager, but that guy definitely should not be in the big leagues.* The clubhouse was quiet after the game. The players were picking at the spread and taking food back to their lockers. Most sat with their back to the clubhouse, so the reporters wouldn't talk to them. Cantos was the exception. He sat facing the gaggle of reporters who stuck their various recording devices inches from his mouth.

"How do you feel about tonight's loss?" asked an overweight radio reporter who looked like he never played a sport in his life.

"How would you feel about it? We had a chance in the ninth, but didn't come through," Cantos replied.

Another reporter asked, "Do you think that the skipper should have pinch hit for Thompson in that spot?"

"How would I know, I'm not the manager. That's his decision. Do I think we had options off the bench? Yes, I do. But like I said, it's not my call," Cantos replied.

There—he said it, plain as day. He felt that Thompson shouldn't be on this team. It wasn't often that a player threw someone under the bus like that—especially when the team had been winning ... and was in first place ... and the name of the team wasn't the New York Yankees. I looked at Thompson's locker and he had left already, leaving a pile of newspapers behind. I never saw him leave. I wondered if he would hear or read about Cantos' comments. If he did, did he even care?

After the increased interest in the Berg card from Cantos and Thompson, I went home that night and examined it again. Snapping it into the holder, I discovered that the effect still occurred. I racked my brain, trying to come up with a reason for the phenomenon. Anticipating my next step, a plan formed in my head.

CHAPTER
17

The next day, I got up early and cooked breakfast for Mom. Smelling the bacon and eggs, she wandered into the kitchen. Jake jumped from her feet to mine, not wanting to miss the falling scraps, which I made sure fell his way.

"Good morning, Van," she said, walking over to give me a hug.

"Hi, Mom." My plan from last night needed her help, so I mustered up the nerve and asked, "Do you think you can do me a favor?"

"Sure, but I need to know what it is before I commit."

"I was wondering if you can have your buddies at the X-ray department zap a picture of something for me?" I asked as spunky as I could.

"What exactly do you want to have X-rayed? You didn't injure yourself last night, did you?"

"Nah, it's nothing like that." I unzipped my backpack. Retrieving the holder, I said, "It's this thing."

"What is it?" she asked and took it from me. Examining it, she shrugged.

"Well, that's just it. I'm not sure *what* it is. I think it's a baseball card holder, but it has some kind of mechanism in it. When I put this card in, it heats up ... watch." I popped in the Berg card. The card heated without fail. "It only happens with my Moe Berg card, it's one that Dad gave me. When I put any other card in, nothing happens."

"Where did you get the holder?" she asked.

"That's the thing. I found it in one of the ballplayer's locker after they left town."

"Shouldn't you give it back?"

"Well, I would have, but now it's almost too late for that. It was during the first series of the season. Players are leaving garbage behind all the time, so I thought he didn't want it. Nobody said anything, so I just kept my mouth shut. I guess I could have had it shipped to the next city for him, but it didn't seem like a big deal, and it was right about the time of Dad's accident. I kind of forgot about it."

"Why do you want it X-rayed?"

"Well, I already had Mr. Han check it with the Geiger counter at school and ..."

"Geiger counter? What's going on with you, Van?"

"I just figured I would take it to him to see if he knew anything about it. He's a freak about his Geiger counter, so he tested it. Look—there are no markings or logos on it." She looked closer. Continuing, I asked, "When have you ever known a company that doesn't put its logos on its products? Never—that's why I'm curious."

"I don't know, Van. I can take it in, but I can't promise you that they will do anything with it."

"Well, I was actually hoping I could go in with you and see for myself."

"I'll check with my friend Debbie and let you know."

"Thanks, Mom."

I finished cooking her breakfast and we ate together. I realized that it had been a while since we sat down together for any kind of meal. We fed Jake some more scraps. I could see that she had developed a great bond with Jake. After breakfast, we moved outside.

We sat on the steps and she said, "Van, how have you been doing lately? I know that baseball has been keeping you busy. Do you miss him?"

"Every day, Mom, every day," I said quietly.

"You know that if you ever need to talk, I'm here. I feel like we're each jumping into our new lives and we don't see very much of each other."

"You know how it is when the Mariners are in town. When they go on the road, we can spend more time together and maybe even take another road trip."

"That's a great idea, let's take a look at the schedule and I'll book something for us."

Jake stood in front of me with a tennis ball, staring with expectant eyes. I got up and tossed the ball while Mom watched us. I could see the loneliness and sadness in her eyes.

"Hey, Mom, do you want to come to the game tonight? Maybe you can call one of your hospital friends to come with you. I might be able to introduce you to Ron Cantos."

"That would be fun. Can you pull it off so late?"

"Yeah, I'll call Fred and make sure he didn't promise the tickets to someone already. Even if he did, I have the final say on who gets them."

I whipped the ball to the far end of the yard and looked over. She was already dialing her cell phone. After a few more tosses, she said, "It's all set, my friend, Debbie, is coming with me tonight. She's a huge fan and can't wait to go to the game."

CHAPTER
18

I arrived at the ballpark around three o'clock. Charlie sat on his old metal stool working a crossword puzzle and looked up as I approached. I wondered if he ever went home.

"Hey, Van, how's the world's best batboy doing today?"

"Ah, come on, Charlie."

"Hey, I gotta tell 'ya. A little while ago, there were two guys that came by here asking a bunch of questions about you—how you got the job and who your friends are. They said they were writing a piece about kids who work in baseball around the country."

"Who were they writing for?"

"They said *Boys Life*, but I don't know. They sure didn't look like *Boys Life* reporters to me. I asked them for their press credentials and they said, 'Sorry to bother you.' Then they left, just like that. Don't worry. I didn't tell them anything. They looked pretty shifty to me."

"They weren't wearing a couple of dark suits and sunglasses, were they?" I asked.

"You've seen them then? That's exactly what they were wearing."

"Charlie, if you ever see them around again, let me know. Those guys have been hanging around a lot. I even saw them at my dad's funeral. They've never done anything to me, but they're always showing up."

"Hey, I've got a couple of buddies that work for the Seattle Police Department. If you ever have any trouble, let me know and I'll send them over to you in a heartbeat."

"Thanks, it sure is nice of you, but like I said, there haven't been any problems. I think we should both keep our eyes open, what do you say?"

"I say that you're one of my favorite kids around here, anything you need, I'll help out anyway I can."

I walked into the tunnel on my way to the clubhouse, trying to put all of the pieces together. It didn't make any sense. What would the Suits want with me? Why were they talking to Thompson? What was Thompson's deal? I wanted to ask Thompson, but I didn't want to risk losing my job. I decided, for now, that I wasn't going to say anything. I was sure there was a logical explanation for everything.

I went to my locker and changed. Out on the field, I soon forgot about the Suits. The other batboys and clubbies milled about. Ricky warmed up with a donut on his bat. One of the perks of the job was that a couple of days during the season, we took some cuts before batting practice.

Ricky was first in the cage and started with a couple of bunts. Then, he let loose and swung away. Gazing at the empty stadium, I saw a flock of screeching seagulls looking for scraps. The constant marine smell was stronger now, without the hotdogs and burgers fighting for smelling rights.

The quiet took some getting used to. During games, the blaring music filled every nanosecond of downtime. Baseball had shifted over the years. Dad would tell me about the Kingdome days, when the game was actually the attraction and the stadium and its ensemble were secondary. Now stadiums were entertainment centers that threw something at your senses at every passing moment.

Ricky finished his cuts and it was my turn. Kicking my cleats into the damp clay, I prepared to rip some balls. I tapped the bat on the plate a couple of times and looked up. The Mariners' coach threw perfect eighty mile-per-hour strikes.

I hit a few fly balls, and then evened things out into a series of line drives. The ball echoed off the outfield wall. The wood bat felt different from the aluminum ones that I had growing up. You got the feeling of a thousand stinging bees in your hand when you fouled off a pitch awkwardly. But, when you connected—oh, what a feeling! I unleashed a roundhouse swing on the next pitch. As soon as I made contact, I knew it had a chance. I watched the arcing ball as it sailed away from me, toward the right field foul pole.

"Stay fair!" I screamed as if I were in a real game.

The ball came down 328 feet away, two feet over the fence in the right field bleachers, just inside the yellow foul pole. I had belted my first home run ball out of a major league ballpark. Ricky high-fived me as I took off my batting helmet.

"Dude, you took one yard. That was awesome, you really should be playing ball."

"I was just lucky. Did you see how late I swung on that pitch? I can't believe it stayed fair." I walked over, picked up my glove and trotted out to shag some balls with the other guys in the outfield. I was still buzzing.

"Hey, kid," a guy sweeping in the aisle called down, "do you want this ball?"

"Yeah, sure," I said, acting like it was no big deal. I caught the ball on a bounce and shoved it in my back pocket. That one was coming home with me.

The real players trickled out for their turn on the field. When I returned to the clubhouse, Ricky was telling everyone that I had hit one out. Greg even seemed impressed. I put my ball on the top shelf of my locker and admired it for a split second.

Grabbing my phone, I walked outside. I had to call Fred and Zoe to tell them about my *Ruthian* feat.

The gates had just opened and the usual rush of early birds streamed in to watch batting practice. I left a message for Fred, and then got a hold of Zoe. The noise level from the crowd increased as I plugged my opposite finger in my ear. "You should have seen it. I hit one out of Safeco!"

"Wow, that's great. Is that hard to do?"

"For me it is. Whatever, it felt pretty cool," I said as I watched an approaching taxi. "One of the cleaning guys threw it back down to me, so I was able to keep the ball." A couple of the Oakland players got out of the cab, I watched as Cantos paid the fare. He walked over as I was talking.

"I can tell by the look on your face that you must be talkin' to your girl. Gimme that phone." Ron grabbed it out of my hand. "Who's this?" Ron asked.

"Zoe. Who's this?" I barely heard through the phone.

"Ron Cantos, I play for Oakland. So, you must be Van's girlfriend."

I was standing there with my mouth open and turning beet red. My hand, still up to my head, held nothing but air.

"I wo ... that. Did you hear ... one out ... park today?"

I strained to hear the garbled voice. Looking at Ron, eyes bugged out, I asked, "What's she saying?" I felt so embarrassed.

"He hit one out? Van Stone took one yard today. I can't believe it," he said. Ron gave me a goofy look, pointing at the phone laughing.

"C'mon," I said.

"Hey, Zoe, I've got to go get ready for the game, I'll give you back to slugger. Hopefully, I'll be able to meet you in person one day." He flipped the phone to me and laughed as he headed toward the gate. Twenty disappointed fans were screaming at him for autographs as he disappeared from view.

"How embarrassing," I said into the phone.

Zoe was laughing on the other end. "You shouldn't be embarrassed, I think it's cool. Besides, you sure did sound excited about it *before* the big shot ballplayer showed up."

"Whatever. Hey, I have to get back inside. You're heading to Eastern Washington tomorrow, right?"

"Yeah, we're only going over for the day. Let's do something on Monday."

"Cool, that'll be great. It's the All-Star break, so I'll have some time off. Gotta run."

I hung up and Charlie waved me in. Back in the clubhouse, things were getting rowdy. Apparently, they had forgotten all about last night's debacle. The music was on and the players were shouting across the clubhouse to each other. As they filed out to the field for batting practice, I noticed that Thompson wasn't here. *Did they send him down to the minors*? I didn't see anything about it in the paper this morning. It wouldn't surprise me if they had. The last of the players jogged out of the clubhouse as I grabbed a drink from the kitchen. When I returned to the main locker area, Thompson was sitting at his locker.

He looked tired, with a scowl on his face, and didn't look up. As always, he wore his perfectly pressed black suit. Quietly, he changed into his uniform, then grabbed his cap and glove, and walked out of the clubhouse without saying a word.

CHAPTER
19

The game featured lots of scoring. The two sides battled back and forth until the ninth inning. Cantos belted a three-run homer to put his team on top for good. Inside the clubhouse, the team celebrated the victory with the usual music and dancing.

Watching Thompson, you couldn't tell if his team won or lost. He had gone oh-for-three with a hit-by-pitch tonight. The rest of the ballplayers looked like they were at Carnival, in Rio, whooping it up and dancing around. As the scene unfolded, I realized that professional ballplayers are just a bunch of kids. The clubhouse cleared out in a hurry, despite the party-like atmosphere. The players looked like they were ready to paint the town red tonight. Thompson was the last out. He showered and dressed in silence. After dressing, he sat at his locker for fifteen minutes reading the pile of newspapers. Without a word, he got up and walked out.

As soon as he left, I stacked his newspapers. I wouldn't dare throw them away. Looking through his locker, I wanted to find anything that would help me figure out this stranger. His glove sat on the lower shelf, a batting glove hung on a side hook and his various t-shirts and sleeves hung in color-coded order. The top shelf was sparse. I found a pen, a note pad and little else. While most of the other guys had lockers that look like they had been hit by a hurricane, Thompson's barely had anything in it. After my survey, I rushed through my usual postgame tasks and left with Ricky at midnight.

The house was quiet when I arrived home. I creaked up the stairs and peeked in at Mom and Jake. A big black wet nose pushed through the crack in the door as I heard the thumping of a tail against the wall.

"Shh, go back to sleep, buddy. I'll see you in the morning."

In my room, I launched Bing and Google. Thompson's name brought up the Director General of the British Broadcasting Company, a radio personality in Los Angeles and some political show on Sirius Radio. About three entries down I read, *Mark Thompson- Oakland A's- MLB Yahoo Sports.*

I clicked the link. A stats page splashed across my screen, filled with Minor League caliber numbers and all too familiar pictures of him. I read his history—drafted in 2008 by the Pittsburg Pirates, traded to Oakland in 2010. I went back to the next link, a baseball reference site. He played ball at Columbia University, *must have had some smarts to go to an Ivy League school.* After that, it was pretty much a dead end.

No great numbers throughout the years, his background was void of anything, other than the fact that he was a mediocre ballplayer that was taking somebody's spot on a Major League roster. The mystery was going to have to wait because I had an early start tomorrow.

Most players looked forward to the All-Star break because they got a few days off. The stars, Cantos included, would head to Minnesota for the mid-season classic. There was no early batting practice today and most of the players arrived on the team bus. It looked like it had been a long night for the team. Cantos went straight to his locker and plopped down in his seat, rubbing his forehead with his eyes closed. A line had formed at the coffee dispenser. Except for the pregame radio show playing over the clubhouse speakers, quiet ruled the locker room.

I was shocked the moment I spotted Thompson. He looked like he had slept in his suit. I had never seen that guy with as much as a hair out of place. He looked around the clubhouse and stopped when he saw me.

"Batboy," he barked.

"Yes sir!" I replied. *Yes sir*? *What's wrong with me*?

"During the game, have someone get my suit dry-cleaned for me."

"Sure, I'll pick it up after you change."

"Thanks."

I spotted Ricky and asked him about getting it done.

"Yeah, it happens every once in a while. We have a place down the road where we send them. They charge like seventy-five bucks for the service, maybe more on Sundays."

"Whoa, that's a chunk of change."

"Just leave it in my locker before you head out to the field and I'll call them for pickup after the game starts," Ricky said.

After the players headed out to take infield, I picked up Thompson's suit. I shoved my hand into each pocket. They were all empty until I got to the back pocket, where I found a folded up parking receipt. Reaching up to set it in his locker, I glanced at the ticket. I felt my body fire its limbic alarms. *It can't be, I know that receipt.* I had seen a hundred of them.

Biotrust 3:00 a.m., dated today.

Memories of Dad flooded back to me. What was a professional baseball player doing at Biotrust in the middle of the night? My hands trembled as I put the receipt on the upper shelf.

I threw his suit into Ricky's locker and collapsed into my seat with my head in my hands. It didn't make any sense. Thompson had come in looking like he hadn't slept all night, and he was at Biotrust at three in the morning. What was his connection with Biotrust? Why was he there in the middle of the night? Summoning my courage, I stood up. I had to get on the field, and I couldn't let Thompson know that I had found the receipt.

I jogged out on the field and tried to act normal. One of the players asked me to warm him up. At least that helped me relax a little bit. I kept my eye out for Thompson while trying to be inconspicuous. After infield, I scanned the stands. Sure enough, the Suits were right there.

Ricky and Greg packed up the travel bags as I tried to concentrate on the game that was taking place in front of me. Cantos struggled at the plate and looked like he didn't even want to be here. Seattle pitching was on a roll and the game moved at a great pace. Thompson sat at the end of the dugout, benched all day. I didn't see any other player interact with him throughout the entire game.

Inside, it was quiet again following their loss. Thompson's newly dry-cleaned suit was hanging in his locker. The players showered and dressed in record time. The clubhouse emptied, leaving Ricky and me to clean. I didn't feel like eating and skipped the spread. Greg had already headed back to the laundry room to do whatever it was that he did back there.

"Ricky, do you know where my dad worked?" I asked.

"Yeah, over at Biotrust."

"Right. Well, I found a receipt in Thompson's suit from their parking garage."

"Maybe he went for a tour. It's a big tourist attraction."

"It had a time stamp on it from three o'clock this morning."

"Oh—that's kind of weird."

"I told you about the Suits that keep showing up, they were here again today. I don't know what to do. It's getting really creepy."

"Have you told anyone about this?" Ricky asked.

"Fred and Zoe know, not about today, but about the other stuff. I'm going to tell my mom about everything when I get home. Maybe she can help me figure out what's going on."

"I'm sure it's nothing. Let's get going on the clubhouse so we can get out of here."

Since it was "get-away-day," we finished the chores quickly. I jumped into the shower and changed at my locker. Stuffing my dirty clothes into my backpack, I noticed a slip of paper that wasn't there before. I pulled it out as if I was picking up a snake. A slight heaviness revealed a key taped to the outside, below that, typed in capital letters was a single word, VAN. I unfolded the sheet and read:

YOU DON'T WANT THE SAME THING TO HAPPEN
TO YOUR MOM THAT HAPPENED TO YOUR DAD. YOU
WILL NOT TALK TO ANYONE ABOUT THIS.
TOMORROW YOU WILL TAKE MOE BERG TO THE FIRST
NATIONAL BANK OF SEATTLE. YOU WILL ASK FOR
THE BANK MANAGER AND DEPOSIT THE CARD INTO
SAFETY DEPOSIT BOX NUMBER 1453. TELL NO ONE—
OR YOU WILL BE SORRY.

CHAPTER
20

I looked around as if that would tell me who put the note in my bag. *Who knew about my Moe Berg card?*

Cantos, Thompson, Greg, Ricky, maybe even Charlie.

What was so important about the card? My mind raced as I stared at the first sentence. My legs weakened, feeling like a mile sprinter depleted of glycogen. *What did this have to do with Dad's accident?* Nothing—they said the accident was just that—an accident. The investigation turned up nothing. *Who was trying to scare me into thinking it was something more?* I grabbed my phone to call Mom and stopped.

TELL NO ONE—OR YOU WILL BE SORRY.

I couldn't tell her.

Ricky called out, "Are you coming, or are you ... Dude, you look like you saw a ghost, what's up?" Ricky asked.

"Uh, nothing ... I, uh, forgot about something I was supposed to do earlier," I lied.

"It must've been pretty important. Are you sure you're okay?"

"Yeah, I'm fine, let's go." I stuffed the note into my backpack and we walked out together. My eyes looked left and right as we walked through the hallway. *Could it be the Suits? No way, they couldn't get into the clubhouse.* A cat jumped down from the top of the security booth and I nearly jumped out of my shoes.

"Man, you need to get some sleep or something. You're as jumpy as a jack-in-the-box," Ricky said.

"No, really, I'm fine. I guess it's been a long home stand. I'll see you after the All-Star break. Text me when you know what time to meet the truck."

I unlocked the car door and checked the backseat before I climbed in. As I turned the key, I laid my head on the steering wheel. I had to get it together and figure this out. I dialed Zoe's number.

"Hi, Van, what's up?" Her voice never sounded better.

"Not much. I just got out of the ballpark. What's up with you?" *Do I tell her about the note?*

"We're on our way back from visiting my cousin's family. I told you I was going there today, didn't I?"

"Oh, yeah, that's right," I replied.

"What's wrong with you? You sound weird," she said.

"Nothing, I'm fine, really. Just a little tired. I think I'm just going to head home and crash." *Great choice of words*, I thought. "I'll talk to you tomorrow. Why don't we get together in the morning?"

"Sure, I'll come over to your place. You better get some sleep."

I pulled out of the parking lot, driving like an old man. My head was on a swivel as I saw things I had never noticed before—a homeless guy holding up a cardboard sign that read "Are You Saved", a warehouse with a nameless truck unloading boxes.

I looked in the rear view mirror and saw a car following me. Looking for the closest side street, I found one just up ahead. Turning right, I realized it was a dead end. It was too late—I had to keep turning. The pursuer continued and a hand rose out of the driver side window. Ricky waved as he passed by and I blew out a sigh of relief. I had to calm down. I jumped as my phone buzzed.

"y r u turning in a dead end" Ricky texted.

Ignoring his text, I pulled out and hurried home.

Mom's car was gone when I arrived. Jake greeted me as I opened the front door. He leaped and planted his huge front paws on my shoulders. Stumbling back, I caught my balance before he pushed me out the door. I grabbed the leash and took Jake to the front yard. My eyes scanned down the street, looking for the Suits or anything else out of place. Everything looked normal.

I sat on the stoop, thinking about what to do next. I had to tell someone. There was no way I could tell Mom. I would endanger her life. Zoe was out of town, so that left Fred. Dialing the phone, I wondered if I was doing the right thing. He answered on the first ring. "Fred, are you doing anything?"

"I'm in the middle of a fight in *Halo Reach*."

"Why did you pick up the phone?"

"Because it's you, bro, wouldn't you do the same for me?"

I hesitated for a second and said, "Yeah, 'course I would. Hey, do you think you can hit pause and come over for a little while?"

"I guess, how come?"

"I want to show you something I got at the clubhouse today."

"Cool, what is it? Did you get some massive tips? I bet you got one of Cantos' bats, didn't you?"

"No, nothing like that—get over here as soon as you can."

"I'm on my way, be there in five."

I went back in with Jake and looked around the house, everything looked normal. I ran up to my room and held my Moe Berg card. I felt the rough edges between my fingers, wondering how such a small thing could be causing so many problems. My eyes stared intensely into the ancient face of Moe Berg, willing it to tell me its secrets. Jake jumped up on the bed and cards went flying.

"Jake, come on. Get off the bed," I said and restacked the cards. The doorbell rang and I jumped, scattering the cards again.

Bounding down the stairs, I slid to a stop in the foyer. Peering through the peephole, I saw Fred and threw the door open.

"Let me see it, what did you get?" he screamed.

I grabbed his arm, pulled him in and locked the door. "Follow me—upstairs."

"Uh, Van? What's wrong with you? You look like you've seen a ghost."

"That's not the first time I've heard that today ... you'll see."

When we got to my room, I pulled out the note. "Read this," I ordered.

After a minute, Fred looked up, his eyes as big as half dollars. The unflappable Fred spoke, "D-D-Dude, this is serious stuff. Where did you find this?"

"It was in my backpack, in the clubhouse. I didn't find it until I was on my way out. I have no idea who put it in there. It had to have happened during the game. That was the only time I was out of the clubhouse for any length of time. I think the bigger question is—who did it?"

"Who do you think?" Fred asked as his voice wavered.

"The only ones in the clubhouse that even know I have a Moe Berg card are Ricky, Cantos and Mark Thompson, the freak I told you about. I can't believe that it would be Ricky, what would be his motive?

"What would be anybody's motive?" Fred asked, talking faster.

"That's what we have to figure out."

"What about your boss, Greg? Didn't you tell me that he's a real pain?"

"I forgot about him. You're right. He was in the clubhouse all day. I'm sure he could have found out something through Ricky. The other thing is, every time I walk into the laundry room, he slams shut a cabinet and locks it. I don't know what he's hiding in there."

Fred read the note again. "Where's the card? Let me see it again."

I pulled it out of the stack and tossed it to him. He examined it closer this time.

"When did your dad give you this card?"

"We were driving to the stadium—on the first day of the season."

"So, between Greg, Ricky, Cantos and Thompson, who is the most likely to have put that note in your locker?"

"I don't know. Cantos played at designated hitter, so he wasn't on the field for defense. Why in the world would he care about this card?

"Why in the world would *anybody* care about the card?" a panicky Fred said.

I continued, "Calm down, we have to think this through. Thompson wasn't even in the lineup today. He sat on the bench the whole game. He could have gone in and out at anytime. There's no way it could be Ricky. He was there when I found it. Either he's the best actor in the world or he doesn't know anything about this ... and I already told you about Greg."

Fred sat on the bed staring at the card. Jake stood up on his hind legs and put his front paws on the bed. He stared at the card with the two of us.

"There's something else. I had to get Thompson's suit dry cleaned today during the game. When I cleaned out his pockets I found a parking receipt for Biotrust."

Fred slowly raised his head. "What?" he said, elongating the word.

"Would you believe at three in the morning? You tell me—why would he be there at three in the morning?"

"I have no idea," Fred half whispered, deep in thought. "I think he has to be our prime suspect. Here's what we need to do. You're going to call the cops, right now. You can't say anything to your mom. Then, I hope this thing will be over—no more guys in suits, no more threats and no more Moe Berg."

"Are you crazy?" I shouted and continued in a softer voice. "I can't do that, what if something happens to my mom? I'm sorry—I not calling the police."

We sat, silently taking it all in. Fred started to say something, but I cut him off.

"What if this Moe Berg card is really important? We have to find out why someone wants it so bad. The last thing I want is for it to fall into the hands of the wrong people."

"I don't know, Van. How could that card contain something that could impact the world?"

"Don't you watch movies? What if it contains the real identity of all the CIA spies, stolen secrets from the military or plans for making a nuclear bomb?"

"Dude, I can get that off the internet—watch ..."

"No! That's all I need now—the government watching me because you pulled up the plans for a nuclear bomb on *my* computer." I continued, "Think about it—what if there's something in here that could harm thousands or millions of people—a program that could wipe out the entire financial system? That would create chaos in the world. Do we want to be responsible for handing that over to the bad guys?"

"You got a point, but what can we do? We're just a couple of kids. This is serious business."

"That is exactly why we can't do anything until we know more about the card," I said.

"Where do we start?" Fred asked.

"My dad gave me the card, so let's start there."

"What was he working on at Biotrust?"

"I have no idea, that's the problem. He couldn't talk about what he worked on. He always changed the subject when I asked him. Do you think that his work could be related to the note?" I asked.

"Think about it, he told you it was valuable. You looked it up and it's not worth anything. I think we need to take a closer look at that card."

CHAPTER
21

F red took the card and examined it closer. "There isn't anything on the outside that looks unusual. Give me one of the other baseball cards."

I handed him a random card and said, "You can see that it's thicker, but that's not unusual with replica cards. Sometimes they would make them on thicker card stock to resemble the cards of the early days."

Fred turned the card repeatedly, looking for a clue. He placed it in the holder. Within about a minute, it heated up. "There's *got* to be a reason for that. Have you searched Google and Bing for the card holder?"

"Yep, nothing. I asked my mom if someone at the hospital could X-ray the card and holder. What do you think about that approach?"

"That's a great idea. When will she be home?"

"She should be here any minute," I said as Jake jumped up and ran downstairs. Fred and I looked at each other. A few seconds later, we heard the front door open. "Don't freak her out or anything. Don't say anything about the note until we figure out what we're going to do. Be calm and let *me* do the talking," I said.

We clambered down the stairs. "Hi, Mom."

"Hi, Mrs. Stone," Fred said with way too much excitement.

"Hi, guys. What are you doing here, Fred? Did you go to the game today?"

"Nah, Van called me as soon as he got home and I came over as fast as I could. Hey, when can you X-ray that card for Van?"

I rolled my eyes. *Great ... good thing Fred listens to me so well.*

She looked at me with a puzzled look. "The card—oh, you mean the thing you were talking about last week?"

"Right," I replied.

"I talked to Debbie about it the other night at the game. She said sure, just come in during an off time when they're not busy," Mom said as she set down her purse and keys. "I didn't tell you yet, but I booked us a couple of nights at Ocean Shores this week. Maybe we can take it in when we get back."

"This week?" I had forgotten all about going out of town. There was no way I could leave now. I had to come up with something good, so I lied, "I thought we were going to do that later in the summer. I told Greg that I would help with some changes we're making in the clubhouse this week, during the All-Star break. I'm sorry, Mom, is there any way we can go to the beach in a couple of weeks?"

"Well, I guess so. I was looking forward to getting out of the city for a while."

"You could always give Aunt Judy a call, I know she's been asking for you to go visit."

"Are you trying to get rid of me?"

"No, of course not. It's just that—I'll be spending a lot of time at the clubhouse this week. We've got a lot of work to do before the next team comes in."

"Oh, all right, maybe I'll give her a call."

"That's cool. Do you think we can go see Debbie tomorrow?"

"I'll call her and find out. I know she's on the night shift tomorrow. Why so urgent?"

"No reason. We're just curious. Who knows, it might be valuable."

"Well, I'll let you know in the morning, I'm tired, I want to go take a bath and get ready for bed. If you guys don't mind, I'm going to disappear."

Fred and I went back up to my room. "Let's do a little research on Biotrust," I said.

Surfing to the Biotrust website, I clicked deeper. "Here we go—a link for projects and partnerships." It listed several pharmaceutical companies and related projects about developing drugs for arthritis, cholesterol and other ailments.

"Look, there." Fred pointed at the screen. I clicked on a link for government partnerships. The website revealed a flowery public relations piece about Biotrust working with the government to keep our country safer.

"What do you think? Could that have something to do with this?" Fred asked while looking at the card.

"I don't know. I *do* know that my dad couldn't talk about what he was working on … sounds like government and national security to me."

I thought for a moment and said, "Thompson was at the facility. There has to be a connection. What I don't get is why a Major League baseball player would want anything to do with Biotrust. Hey, wait a minute. I remember finding pieces of newspaper with the stock listing for Biotrust highlighted."

"What would that have to do with the Berg card?"

"I have no idea. But clearly, he was watching the value of the company."

"Why wasn't your dad working right before the accident?"

"We didn't really talk about it too much. His bosses told him to take a little vacation. They put his project on hold. He was even talking about getting out completely and starting his own consulting company."

"Do you think there's any connection between your dad and the card holder?"

"How could there be? Thompson had the holder in his locker. It was my first series on the job. Thompson and my dad never knew each other," I said and stared blankly at the wall.

"Van, I just thought of something. What if getting the job was a setup. I mean, think about it. You're nobody, and then all of a sudden, you're in the big leagues. Doesn't it seem a little too perfect?"

"Yeah, but I wrote an essay to get the job. How would anyone know that I was going to enter the essay contest?" I replied.

"We don't know how far reaching the government can be!" Fred said.

We sat, silent. The silence gave way to the pelting of rain on the window. The heat of the day helped to create an unstable air mass. As it mixed with the upper level cooler air, lightning sparked in the distance, followed by a low rumble.

I continued, "We need to concentrate on finding out what Biotrust was working on and what Mark Thompson's role is in all of this. What keeps gnawing at me is that he plays on a Major League baseball team. How could he be playing baseball and be involved in some kind of conspiracy? The millions of dollars involved—plus the fans. How can a team have even one player on their roster that they don't believe in as a ballplayer?"

"Didn't you tell me that he doesn't put up the numbers, yet he's still there?" Fred asked.

"Yeah, exactly, but think about the implications if that were true. You're lying to your fan base. You're lying to your investors. How could they ever get away with that?"

"Didn't the Pittsburgh Pirates lie to their fans just so they could make more money?" Fred asked. "It happens all the time in sports or any other business, bro."

"That was different. They told the fans they were losing money and couldn't afford a quality product, so the fans had a choice to support the team or not. What the fans didn't know was that the owners were making money hand-over-fist," I said.

"So, what should we do?" Fred asked.

"I think we're safe for now. Nobody is expecting the card until tomorrow. Besides, Thompson and Cantos are both out of town. That only leaves Greg here in Seattle. That gives us a day to figure out a plan. Let's sleep on it and see what we come up with tomorrow."

"Good idea."

We headed downstairs and I said, "Let's get together with Zoe tomorrow and see what she has to say. Do you want me to give you a ride home?"

"Yeah, that'd be sweet."

Walking outside, I looked down the street. Everything was different now. Nothing seemed the same—the cars parked on the street, the sound of the rain hitting the metal gutters, a tire screeching in the distance—I analyzed everything now. We drove the few minutes to Fred's without much conversation. I dropped him off and turned around for home.

Being alone in the car, I felt more isolated than ever. I thought it was lonely after Dad died, but this was worse than that. I didn't have anyone to turn to and I might be putting others in danger.

I pulled onto a main street. Suddenly, two halogen lamps materialized and a car fell in place behind me, matching my speed.

"Don't be paranoid," I said to an empty car.

An intersection approached, I made an unnecessary right to test the path of the tailgater. The mystery car shadowed my movement. An influx of adrenalin accelerated my heartbeat as I advanced toward the next turn. I made a left and stared at my rearview mirror, willing away the reflection of the beams. The car slowed and then continued on its straight path.

I took a deep breath. "Get a grip, Van," I said to no one. My house appeared ahead, a temporary sanctuary. Tonight's sleep would be anything but restful.

CHAPTER
22

The morning arrived too early. I dusted the cobwebs out of my brain as I tried to convince myself that the past twenty-four hours was a dream. All night, I struggled with the looming decision. I had to protect Mom and my friends. Yet, I had to uncover the meaning behind the card and its connection to Biotrust.

My phone buzzed, Fred had texted asking where to meet. Replying to Fred and Zoe, I offered up the nearby Top Pot Doughnuts. Mom was still asleep, so I left a note and tiptoed out with my backpack containing the holder and card.

Fred was stuffing a doughnut in his mouth when I arrived.

"Van, when were you going to tell me about this?" Zoe asked.

I shot Fred a glance. "Thanks, buddy ... I'm glad you're looking out for me."

"What?" Fred exclaimed with his mouth full and arms extended.

"Zoe, you have to tell me what Fred said. We know he has a habit of changing the story around a bit."

She proceeded to fill me in on a surprisingly detailed and accurate picture of what had transpired. "... so, like I said, when were you going to fill me in on this?"

"That's what we're doing here. The first question is, how seriously do we take this threat?"

"I think that you and your mom are the ones in danger," Fred said. "They don't even know we exist."

"Let's not forget about the Suits. They saw you guys with me at the memorial service. Oh, and you," I pointed directly at Fred, "chased them to their car, where they supposedly 'ID'ed' you, remember?"

"Oh, yeah—well, how was I supposed to know?"

"They also saw me at the ballpark. I'll never forget the weird look they gave me." Zoe shuddered. "And Fred, I'm sure they couldn't have missed your face-plant. They definitely know who we are."

"Regardless, for the time being, I think we're okay," I said. "We have a window of opportunity here to find out the meaning of the Berg card. We need to decide our next move."

"Why don't you just go drop off the card?" Zoe asked.

Fred and I filled her in on our thoughts from last night. We all arrived at the same conclusion. The consequences of dropping it off could be worse than hanging on to it, at least until we knew more about it.

"All right—agreed," I said. "The next question, what do we do about the bank?"

"How 'bout I scope out the place?" Fred suggested. "Maybe I go in and open a checking account or something. I can ask to see the bank manager because I'm considering becoming a new customer."

"Not a bad idea, but I have a *better* idea." I waited with two sets of eyes staring at me.

"*What?*" the unison response came after a couple of seconds.

"I'm thinking that I go and make the deposit, but I leave another card in the box, not the Berg card. We'll definitely find out how serious this thing is by their response. I can leave one of Cantos' cards. If Thompson's behind this, we should hear about it right away."

"That's brilliant!" Fred said.

"What if Greg is the one putting you up to this?" Zoe asked.

"If that's the case, it wouldn't matter whose card I put in there, he'll see that it's the wrong one and make his next move. I'll still have the Berg card and as long as I have what he wants, I can keep control."

"You mean WE would still have what he wants, bro. We're in this with you," Fred said. Zoe nodded her head in agreement.

"You guys know that you don't have to do this," I said.

"Van, I trust your judgment," Zoe said. "If your dad's work has anything to do with this, I know that we couldn't stop you anyway. So, we might as well help you out. We don't want you going at it alone."

"What she said," Fred added, pointing at Zoe.

"I talked to my mom about her trip to my aunt's house, over in Pullman. I hope she'll get out of town where she'll be safer, without knowing about any of this."

"Hey, you can crash at my place," Fred said.

"Perfect, and the All-Star Game is Tuesday night, maybe we can *all* crash at your place for the game?" I asked.

"Yeah, that'd be sweet. After the game, we can play *Rock Band* all night," Fred said.

"Great," Zoe said sarcastically.

"Next thing, I think we should go visit Biotrust. We can schedule a tour. I'll tell them that I'm preparing a presentation for my school and thought it would be nice to honor my dad. We would showcase their company and talk about all the good they do around the world."

"Another great idea—how do you do it?" Fred asked with an amazed look.

"Fred, since when have you become such a 'yes' man?" Zoe asked. "Your nose is getting a little brown—but I do agree it *is* a good idea."

"I'm going to call and see if we can get in there tomorrow. Meanwhile, we need to decide on what time we should go to the bank. The way I see it, the closer it is to closing time, the better," I said.

"I'm ready whenever you are," Fred said.

"Let's meet at the bus stop at four-thirty. Taking the bus will be better than driving. We don't have to worry about parking and we'll be around more people."

"Three could be a crowd," Zoe said. "I think I'll pass and let you two go. We don't even know if they'll let anyone other than you into the safety deposit box room."

"You're probably right. Fred, we'll meet at the bus, and Zoe, plan on meeting at my house around seven to go to the hospital with us."

"Sounds like a plan," Zoe said.

"Just remember, keep your eyes open and your head on a swivel. If anything looks out of place, text me and get around other people in a hurry," I said.

"Don't worry. I can take care of myself," Zoe replied.

CHAPTER
23

At 4:15, Fred walked up to the bus stop, dressed in a gray hoodie, black jeans that sank below his waist and carried a beaten up backpack. He stopped a few feet away from me and held up a cardboard sign:

Lost job
Hungry
Anything will help

"What do you think of my disguise?"
"You look normal, 'bout the same as you do every day."

"C'mon, don't you think it's a great idea?"

"Actually, it is pretty good. Dude, what's that smell?"

"Oh, I cooked up some bacon, threw the grease in the yard and rolled around in it to give the disguise a dose of reality."

"Great, a homeless person that smells like bacon. Very realistic," I said. "When we get there, you can hang outside the bank. Keep your eyes open for anyone suspicious, especially the Suits." I squinted, looking at his head. "Dude, is that grease, dripping down your forehead? Did you pour it in your hair?"

"A little," Fred said. The lard oozed into his eyes. "Ah, it stings!" he said as he blotted it with his sleeve.

Shaking my head I said, "Here's our bus, let's go."

We climbed on and looked for seats away from each other. Fred sat on one of the sideways seats between to two older women, while I moved toward the back. After about ten seconds, the women got up and moved to other seats. Fred sat with his head drooping forward and mumbling to himself.

I texted him as we rumbled toward downtown:

"When we get there I will go str8 in. u wait outside. I don't think we should talk"

After a few seconds, I watched the supposed jobless person pull out his cell phone and read the text.

I texted him again:

"Way 2 stay in character"

I watched as Fred dug through his ratty backpack and flipped over his sign. I could see him writing, then he held up the sign, which read:

Just lost my job
Still have my cell phone

I texted:

"lol, k let's get back into this. No jokes"

The bus pulled up a block from the bank. Fred shuffled out first and wandered down the street. I stepped off the bus and took a deep breath, inhaling a lung full of exhaust. As the air cleared, the unique mix of salty sea air and coffee drifted toward me. Big crowds packed the sidewalks on this sunny Monday afternoon. No one appeared to be in any particular hurry. Some were walking with a purpose and others were just strolling while enjoying the weather.

My eyes scanned the crowd as I moved toward the bank. I carried my backpack in front of me, my arms wrapped around it as if it were a baby. On high alert, I looked for anyone suspicious. For a moment, I doubted my plan and questioned whether we should go to the police. Just then, someone bumped my arm. Grabbing my backpack tighter, I spun my head—my eyes wild.

"Sorry, dude. I didn't mean to run in to you," the dreadlock headed stranger said and moved on.

Fred had found a spot right outside the bank entrance. He had pulled a coffee cup out of the trash and was working the part. I arrived at the entrance. The outside of the bank was not impressive. A typical storefront glass bank, I guess I was expecting some distinguished old-time architecture that you find in so many buildings in downtown Seattle. I took one last look at Fred, he was shooing away a dog that was licking his pant leg.

A nervous tension settled in as I opened the front door. A tall uniformed security guard greeted me as I entered. The lobby was modern institutional, no character or feeling to it. There were only two tellers behind the counter and three customers, two stood at the counter and one in line. On the left side, two offices sat empty. I walked up to a stiff, older woman at the information desk.

"How can I help you?" she asked with a nasally voice. Her tight collar buttoned up to her neck. She looked over the top of her glasses that were centimeters from falling off her long skinny nose.

"I need to speak to the bank manager, please."

"Is he expecting you? Do you have an appointment?"

"No, Ma'am, I was told to ask for him."

"One moment, please. Have a seat in the waiting area— and your name?"

"Van Stone."

I sauntered to a waiting area that consisted of a very comfortable looking chair. The type of chair that made you look silly when you tried to climb out of it. It was a grand plot, designed to transfer power and control to the person still standing. I decided to continue standing.

After a few minutes, a rather portly man dressed in a cheap brown suit, strolled up to me. His bulbous red face was one mixed with an unsure smile and a nervousness that resembled a mouse trying to complete a maze. Without making eye contact he said, "Hi, my name is Mr. Warfield. How can I be of service to you, Mr., uh, Stone?"

"I have something to put into safety deposit box number 1453."

"Ah, yes, I was expecting you. I'm so glad you made it in today."

"Why?" I asked, hoping to get some insight on what was going on.

"What's that? Oh, no reason in particular. I received a note signed by the box owner that said you would be coming in and to allow you to make a deposit into the box," he said as sweat rolled over his jowls despite the cool temperature. "Please, follow me."

I fell in step behind him as we moved toward a door to the right of the tellers. It felt as if everyone in the bank was watching me. I saw the two employees leaning toward each other, whispering. The manager pounded some numbers into a lock mechanism and a metallic click followed. He yanked the door open and led me down a narrow corridor. After punching a code into a second lock, he pushed the door inward. We walked into a gleaming room with bright lights that reflected off the shiny metal walls. The temperature felt like it had dropped twenty degrees. A lone high table stood in the middle of the room. Two doors led into private offices on either side.

"Do you have the key, Mr. Stone?"

Fumbling with my backpack, I pulled out the note. Mr. Warfield stared at my hands as I peeled the key from the paper. "I've got it." I glanced at him and he quickly looked away. He led me to a wall of small doors with keyholes.

"Please insert your key into box 1453," he said.

I did as instructed and stepped back. He removed a key ring from his belt and with a quick turn of his key, he removed the box and set it on the table.

"You can use either of those offices to conduct your business. I will be waiting for you here."

I picked up the long, heavy metal box with two hands and walked to the door on the left. The manager shuffled over and opened the door, letting it close behind me.

The room was no bigger than a small closet. A single chair and tiny desk filled most of the space. I started to shake, from either the cold or my nerves. Licking my lips, I realized my mouth had gone dry. Questions filled my mind.

I hesitated for a moment, wondering if I was doing the right thing—or was I putting people I love in danger. I couldn't shake that glimmer of self-doubt, imbedded deep within. The unknown significance of the Berg card snuffed out that small flame of doubt—then it hit me like a brick.

Dad's words as we drove to the ballpark on opening day, repeated in my head.

"You should always hang on to this card—it's special."

I was not going to give up the Berg card that easily. I had to find out the meaning behind the card. I knew I was doing the right thing. With renewed vigor, I lifted the cold, elongated lid and saw the simple note:

NOT A WORD TO ANYONE

A chill ran down my spine. I unzipped my backpack and pulled out the Cantos card. Folding the note, I stuffed it into my pocket and placed the card in the box. Hesitating, I stared at the face of Cantos.

"This is for you, Dad," I said and slammed the lid shut. A tremendous sense of empowerment and confidence flooded my body. Picking up the box, I threw open the door and walked out into the bright lights of the main room.

"Did you find everything to be to your satisfaction, Mr. Stone?"

"You better believe it," I asserted.

The manager led me back through the corridors of the bank. We walked into the main area, where different customers mingled in the lobby. I focused on a straight path to the door as the manager spoke.

"Come back and see us again soon."

"Not if I can help it," I whispered.

The security guard opened the door for me and I bolted into the sunshine. Fred sat against a wall and slowly climbed up as I walked by him on my way to the street corner. While waiting for the light to change, a stench overtook me. Others at the corner moved away. Looking in the direction of the smell, I saw Fred standing about three feet from me.

"Dude, I have to get out of these clothes," he whispered loudly. The mixture of the bacon grease, warm sun and perspiration had Fred smelling as if he'd been on the street for a week.

"At least you fit the part. Maybe we should take separate buses home so no one will see us together."

"You're just trying to get rid of me because I reek."

The bus pulled up and I climbed on. Behind me, Fred was trying to climb aboard.

"No way, buddy," the driver yelled, "get yourself a shower before you get on my bus."

"But ... I have a bus pass!" Fred screamed as the driver slammed the door in his face. I looked back to see Fred running after the bus as we drove away.

CHAPTER
24

It was a little after seven when a squeaky-clean Fred showed up at the house.

"Ugh, what is that? Are you wearing perfume?" I asked.

"Lilac, it's the only thing my mom said would get rid of the smell," Fred complained. "Oh, and thanks for bailing on me, buddy."

"What was I supposed to do? If I had gone to bat for you, they would have known we were together. So, how *did* you get home?" I asked sheepishly.

"I took a cab. At first, the driver wouldn't let me in. I had to give him a ten up front to prove I could fork over the fare—and I had to promise him a good tip, too. You know, it wasn't so bad in front of the bank. I actually scored seventeen bucks."

"Seventeen bucks! How'd you do that, I was only in there for about fifteen minutes?"

"One guy paid me a fiver to watch his dog while he went in to make a deposit. The rest of the time, I was singing and crackin' jokes. I kinda drew a crowd."

"You are unbelievable. Well, thanks for doing it."

"No problem, it was fun. Next time, though, I think I'll skip out on rolling in bacon grease. That rank smell got so nasty. I don't think I can eat that stuff for at least a month."

Mom yelled from upstairs, "I'll be down in a minute."

"Now remember, don't mention anything about what we did today."

"Just chill, our secret is safe with me."

The doorbell rang, Jake barked a couple of times and we both jumped. I ran over to look out the window and saw Zoe, impatiently looking up and down the street.

I nodded to Fred and he opened the door. Zoe lurched in and then slammed the door shut.

"What's wrong with you?" I asked.

"After this morning, I've been looking over my shoulder at every turn," she whispered. "I never would have expected to react this way, but I guess since I've been on my own today, I've had way too much time to think about things."

"Well, did you see anything strange or out of place?" Fred asked.

"You mean from the inside of my room? Because that's where I spent pretty much the whole day, until I walked over here."

Mom came down the stairs and saw our little huddle. "What's going on with you three? I don't think I've ever heard you guys so quiet."

"Nothing, Mrs. Stone," Fred responded too quickly.

"Oh, hi, Mrs. Stone," Zoe said.

It's a good thing nobody is acting guilty, I thought while glaring at the two of them. With an innocent voice, I asked, "Are you ready to go, Mom?"

"Let me grab my purse and we'll leave. I wish you people would tell me what was so important about this. I'm starting to get a little concerned."

"It's nothing. We just want to see what makes this card tick. It's probably no big deal. I hope we're not getting you into trouble at the hospital."

"I wouldn't be doing it if you were. Debbie said it would be fine. She said that she's X-rayed all sorts of strange things over the years—an old Etch-a-Sketch, a Cabbage Patch doll and even her Ouija board. So, I guess she understands what your curiosity is all about."

While Mom was locking the door, I glanced down the street. I couldn't be sure, but four houses down, it looked like the same unmarked sedan sat darkened at the curb. Getting into her car, Mom was talking with the other two about their summer plans and didn't notice my uneasiness. Driving away, I breathed a sigh of relief when I saw that no one had followed us onto the main road.

"Van, I talked to Aunt Judy today. She's so excited that I'm coming. I'm going to leave early tomorrow morning. Are you sure I can't talk you into coming with Jake and I?"

"Aw, Mom, you know I would love to come, but with the extra work this week, there's no way I can," I answered. A wave of relief passed through me—she was going out of town.

We arrived at the hospital. Mom told us to hang back for a couple of minutes. She scurried into the department. There were no sign of wheelchairs or stretchers in the hallway. It was a good sign when Debbie and Mom came out to the lobby, looking relaxed and laughing.

"So, what's the big mystery, Van?" Debbie asked.

"Just a couple of trinkets—nothing really. We thought it would be cool to see what they look like inside."

"I'm always ready to help another aspiring *Wilhelm Roentgen*—all in the name of science. Let's go zap 'em."

We followed her into the X-ray department. Mom stopped to talk to a couple of people on the way. She was moving on and developing a life outside of her lost relationship. I felt happy for her and now I understood why she spent so much time volunteering at the hospital. Debbie led us into the X-ray room and I pulled out the card with the holder.

"I've never X-rayed anything like this before, and believe me I've X-rayed lots of strange things," she said as a giggle formed. "There was this one time—oh, never mind, I shouldn't be talking about that. Let me take a look at what you brought."

I handed them over, filled with anticipation about what kind of secrets we were about to uncover. "Could these things do any damage to the X-ray machine, or is there any chance that the X-rays could do any damage to the card?"

"There's no chance that you can harm the machine, and unless there is old fashioned photographic film in there, we aren't going to cause any damage to your mystery items."

She placed the items on the X-ray table and swung the big machine around so that it was hovering right above the devices.

"Everybody needs to step out of the room while I shoot the picture."

We all crowded through the doorway and heard the whir and beep as the radiation beamed toward the items. I found myself holding my breath as if something tragic were about to happen.

"That's one set," Debbie called out. "I'll get a lateral view now, just give me a sec."

A final sound emitted from the room and she gave the all clear. We walked back in while Debbie was removing the film cassette from the table. Apparently, the operation was a success. She opened a panel in the wall and placed the exposed cassette in the compartment that led to the adjoining dark room.

"It takes about forty-five seconds to process the pictures, and then there will be no more mystery," Debbie said as she left us.

The three of us stood in the dimly lit room. Nobody said a word. I heard the tick, tick, tick of the old battery powered clock as its second hand rotated around its face. It felt like the seconds were getting longer as we waited.

Fred broke the silence. "Hey, Van, try zapping a picture of my hand while we wait."

"Yeah, or better yet, let's take an X-ray of your head to check for the size of your brain," I said.

Zoe snickered as Debbie called from the other room, "All right guys, come over here."

We herded into a small room that barely fit the four of us. A film viewer brightly lit the dark space. A large device resembling a heavy-duty copy machine, awakened from its slumber. A dark, flimsy film gradually rolled out of the machine. I felt a sudden rush of adrenalin course through my insides. The X-ray emerged painstakingly slow. It dropped down and Debbie retrieved the plastic.

"Let's see here …" She snapped the film onto the viewer.

I stared, trying to make sense of what I was seeing. The outline of the card holder was apparent. Within centimeters of the edge ran a bright white line. It continued on all sides and through the middle, looking like a squared off number eight. The rest of the holder was nothing but darkness.

I changed my focus to the Berg card. Once again, I barely saw the outline of the card. At the top and bottom of the card were two very small white rectangles. A very thin line ran the length of the card, connecting the two rectangles. A square object that was about one inch on each side interrupted the line. Inside, I saw several white, short strips, which looked like a picket fence, on one border.

The viewer illuminated our bewildered faces. Fred spoke first, "Well, there's definitely something in there. Any ideas?"

"The bright white you see everywhere is metal," Debbie said, pointing to the X-ray.

"What is that thing in the card?" Zoe asked.

"I have no idea," Debbie admitted.

I stared at it, just as puzzled. "The small rectangles on the ends look like contacts. If you place the card in the holder, they would rest against the metal. Maybe the holder is some kind of battery to operate the card?"

"What do you mean by operate?"

I explained the phenomenon to Debbie and she asked, "Nothing happens, except that it heats up?"

"That's right."

"The way I see it," Zoe interjected, "there's something missing."

We all looked at her, waiting for an explanation.

"It's simple. There's another card out there somewhere. The holder has the same circuit in both halves. When that circuit is complete, maybe this thing does whatever it's supposed to do."

"*What*?" Fred jumped in. "When did you become an expert in circuitry?"

"It just so happens that my dad is an electrical engineer. Anyway, that doesn't even matter. It's just common sense."

"She's right," I said, "that has to be it. We still need to find out what it does—and who has the other half."

"Well, guys, I can't really help you anymore, I just take the pictures. It doesn't make much sense to me. If I were you, I would dig that thing out of the card and have someone take a look at it. You can take the film with you." Debbie pulled the radiograph off the viewer and shoved them into a big mustard colored envelope. Then she whispered, "Don't tell anybody where you got these from."

We hustled out of the small room and thanked her for the help. Mom was still chatting up a storm as we got back to the main hallway.

"You guys are done already?"

"Yep, we've got everything we need," Fred said and led the way.

"Did you find anything interesting?"

"We'll talk about it in the car," I said as we stepped out of the hospital doorway. We walked silently, lost in thought. After climbing in, Mom started the car and said, "Okay, people. What's going on? You guys are a little too quiet, especially you, Fred." Her eyes glared at me, in the rear view mirror.

"We're not much closer to solving our mystery," Fred responded.

"If anything, we're probably further away than when we started," I added.

We drove on as I gave her a watered down version of what we saw on the X-ray. After about ten minutes of taking it all in, Mom said, "Doesn't sound like a big deal to me. I guess it's time to move on to the next big mystery of the summer."

Zoe looked at me with eyes that asked if I was going to tell my mom the whole story. Fred saw the exchange and shook his head.

"You're probably right," I agreed. "No big deal. Is anybody up for some ice cream on the way home?"

CHAPTER
25

During the night, I tossed and turned thinking about the events of the day. Had anyone discovered the wrong card? What had the X-rays told us about the Berg card? At least I was comforted in knowing that Mom would be over three hundred miles away. She would be safe.

Mom left at dawn. The house was quiet without her and Jake. The phone rang.

"Van—bad news." It was Fred.

"What?"

"My mom made a dentist appointment for me at 10:45 this morning. She won't let me get out of it. I can't make the Biotrust tour."

"That's okay, Zoe's coming with me."

"I know, but I wanted you to have an extra set of eyes to scope out the place."

"Don't worry, we'll be fine. Let's meet at the coffee shop this afternoon and we can give you a recap of our tour. Don't forget, my mom's in Pullman, so I'll be crashing at your place for the next couple of nights."

"Sweet, let's make sure Zoe stays over tonight, too. Peace out—watch your back at Biotrust."

The phone clicked off. I grabbed my camera and hid the backpack with the devices in the dirty clothes bin. On the drive to Zoe's, I called Mom. She was already to Colfax, with only about a half hour to go. That was a relief. She'll be with family soon, which was better protection than what I could offer. When I arrived at Zoe's, she walked out with a note pad and a video camera, looking like she hadn't slept.

"Rough night?" I asked.

"A little … I got hit with a lot to think about yesterday. I'm not sure if we're handling this the right way. I trust you and I believe in you more than anything, but I just can't wait until this is over so we don't have to keep looking over our shoulders."

"I know the feeling. I hardly slept last night, too." I looked down at my feet, trying to find the right words. "Thanks for believing in me. The last thing I want to do is hurt you, or Fred, or my mom. Deep down inside, I feel that we're doing the right thing."

Unconsciously, my arms raised and wrapped around her. Pulling in, I gave her a brief squeeze. A reassuring embrace that felt so natural. "I won't let anything happen to you," I said and released to an awkward silence.

She smiled at me and said, "I know."

"Let's get to Biotrust," I said sheepishly.

Driving to Biotrust, my thoughts turned to Dad. He took this same route every day. The memories of him mixed with the weight of the situation and the urgency to resolve it. We crossed under the interstate and started up Beacon Hill. The surroundings changed from cars and concrete, to a lush hillside with trees bordering the sides of the road. I slowed the car as a sick feeling crept through my insides. Uncontrollably, my body stiffened, my hands, now white knuckled, turned to a pool of sweat.

"What's wrong, Van?" Zoe asked with a concerned look on her face.

We were about three quarters of the way up the hill when I pointed out a side street.

"Right here. This is where it happened," I said.

At once, Zoe's face changed to one of understanding.

"This was where my dad's accident happened," I said. I had never really thought about it before, the exact location of the accident. It was on his route to Biotrust. We passed the spot in silence.

I thought about Mom and about what it must have been like when she drove up here, after the accident. I imagined the flashing lights, emergency vehicles and his crumpled car loaded on to a flatbed, destined for the scrap heap. I wondered how many people that lived around here even knew that a great dad had died on their road.

A blaring horn snapped me out of my fog and Zoe screamed, "Watch out!" I slammed on the brakes as I realized that I was rolling through a flashing red light. I gave a weak wave to the honking car and let him pass. Silence dominated the remainder of our drive to Biotrust.

CHAPTER
26

Driving up to the parking garage, I imagined Thompson doing the same, at three in the morning. I punched the button on the kiosk and a ticket spit out. Checking the date and time, I saw that it was accurate to the second. Thompson was definitely here in the middle of the night. I went up the ramp into the semi-darkness and pulled into a visitor spot.

The garage was typical, with security cameras mounted at each of the corners. We walked back into the sunlight and approached the main entrance. The building was your run of the mill monolith, a tribute to the profits of the very lucrative biotech industry. Gleaming reflective windows climbed several stories high and over four hundred feet across. I saw my reflection bouncing back at me from three directions in the angled glass of the building. I felt like an ant under a magnifying glass, as if the building was watching me.

I pulled on the huge main door with a heavy tug and stumbled backward slightly, not expecting it open so easily. A cool blast of air met us as we walked into a retro space age lobby. The waiting area had egg shaped seats like those that you would find in an old 1970's movie. The lobby was empty except for a single receptionist who sat at an immense glass desk. She was dressed like the employees in *Tomorrowland*, at Disneyland, and wore a smile that appeared plastered to her face. A giant digital screen ran the width of the room behind her, extolling the virtues of the Biotrust mission.

"Good morning, Mr. Stone," she said with an even broader smile. For a second, I thought she might not be real.

"Good Morning. We're here to see Mr. Barron," I replied, surprised that she knew my name.

"Yes, of course, we were expecting you." She looked at Zoe and asked, "Who might I have the pleasure of meeting today?"

"I'm Zoe Harper. I'm helping Van with his project."

"Of course you are, dear. Before your tour begins, I will need to check you in. Zoe, please step up to this camera and place your chin on the pedestal. I will take a picture of your eye for security precautions. I watched Zoe do as instructed. A high-pitched beep emitted from the camera and she was done.

"Mr. Stone, if you will?"

I switched places with Zoe. On the beep, an invisible infrared light traced across my eye, and then the scan was complete.

"Excellent. It won't be but a moment before Mr. Barron will arrive to conduct your tour. You may have a seat, if you would like."

Zoe and I wandered over to the egg shaped chairs, but didn't sit down. "Pretty high-tech stuff around here, don't you think?" she asked.

"Yeah, they've been using the retinal scans ever since they moved into this new facility."

A door flew open and a rotund, balding man shouted out, "So good to see you again, Mr. Stone." He thrust his hand into mine and shook it vigorously. *See me again*? I thought. I didn't know this guy, unless he had put on a hundred and fifty pounds since I last saw him. He wasn't someone I remembered seeing at the memorial service either, but there was a lot of detail I didn't recall about that day.

"Ah, and you must be Ms. Harper, I presume." His voice was too loud from a foot away.

"Yes, that's me, but you can call me Zoe."

"Great, I hate all the formalities that I must abide by around here. Welcome to our humble facility. My name is Len Barron, Vice President of Media Relations. There are many exciting advancements developed at Biotrust that I am sure you must be eager to see. Let us be going right away. Van ... oh, I am sorry, is it okay if I call you Van?"

"Yeah, of course."

"Great! Follow me, Van and Zoe, and let's see what secrets lay waiting behind these doors."

We followed in step behind him. Zoe glanced at me and we stifled a laugh. I looked down onto his balding head from about a foot and a half above. He was almost as round as he was tall. His white lab coat flew up behind him, like a duster in an old western. Before I knew it, he was a few steps ahead of me. His agility and quickness did not correlate well with the rest of his characteristics.

He faced us, noticed Zoe with her video camera, and stopped on a dime. "One little detail I must ask you to do for me. I am afraid you will have to leave your cell phones and video camera with the receptionist. We do not allow photography of any kind on the campus."

We turned, and the receptionist materialized at my back, holding a box for our electronics. I didn't even see her come up behind us.

"Thank you. Sorry about the inconvenience," Mr. Barron said.

He twirled around and stood on his toes, putting his eye on level with a glass dome. A quick beep and the door swooshed open.

We walked into a sterile corridor that connected the main facility to the lobby. Small rectangular windows ran near the ceiling on one side, allowing the sunlight to penetrate the hallway.

At the end of the corridor, Mr. Barron surrendered to another retinal scan. A *Star Trek* like door slid open to reveal an immense structure. The ceiling soared four floors high and displayed a nighttime scene of stars, the planets and the moon, in its current phase. Each side contained a walkway that led into a row of individual offices on four different floors. On our level, we looked down into what would be an atrium, if this were a hotel or cruise ship. Scientific workbenches, bright portable lighting, refrigeration systems and just about every other gadget that a geek could imagine, filled the main floor, one level down.

A booming voice broke our gaze. "Welcome to the heart of *Biotrust*," Mr. Barron said, waving his arm across the scene as if he were the ringmaster in a circus. He extended out his pronunciation of Biotrust to add a dramatic flair.

"What goes on down there?" Zoe asked.

"That is the preliminary lab for most of our ideas, where we put together prototypes and mock-ups of actual projects. The area is the size of two football fields, although our staff doesn't have much time for games." He laughed at his own joke. After seeing that no one laughed with him, he gathered himself and continued, "The nearest portion is where we complete our initial designs and toward the back, we will find actual projects nearing completion."

"What kind of projects do you have going on now?" I asked.

"All sorts of things," he said enthusiastically. "If you look to the left, you'll see that those scientists are designing a combat helmet. The new guts of the helmet will provide increased protection. If we are lucky, we might even be able to witness them conduct the testing. That is, if you like to see things blow up!" His immense midsection jiggled as his voice moved up several octaves.

"Here is the best part. After the helmet stands up to our rigorous testing, we will outfit it with a special material we have developed which functions as a camera. We are working very closely with the government on this project. Soon, every commander will be able to sit behind a monitor and watch the progress of each of his soldiers, just like playing a multi-player video game."

"Wow, that's impressive. Do you do much work for the government?" I asked.

"I am proud to say that we are working tirelessly in cooperation with the Department of Defense to make our country a safer place."

"What goes on behind those doors?" Zoe asked while pointing to the higher floors.

"That is where our ideas are born. Our inventors and scientists dream up their ideas and pass it down to the floor for the engineers to develop.

"That's where my dad worked. He was on the top floor. Can we see his office?"

"Of course you can, however, please understand, we have given the office to another scientist."

We entered the nearest elevator. "Your website talks about pharmaceuticals, where is that work done?" I asked as we rode to the fourth floor.

"Oh, I see you have done your homework. As you can imagine, security is our main objective. That part of our facility is only accessible through the lower level. You see, the main floor down there is actually below ground level. We keep our higher risk projects isolated from the general public."

"What kind of projects are you working on that are so dangerous?" Zoe jumped in.

"Oh, it's not dangerous. We must keep sterile conditions for many of the wonderful cures that we are working on for diabetes, arthritis, cholesterol and cancer."

"Will we be able to see that area?" Zoe asked.

"Well, it is really not that interesting, just a bunch of scientists stooping over their Petri dishes. Unfortunately, we need to make arrangements about a week in advance to take the general public into that area."

We stepped out of the elevator and I saw that the moon on the ceiling had inched across the fake nighttime sky since we first came in. Mr. Barron said, "Ah, you have noticed our moving nightscape. You see, we work around the clock, here at Biotrust. During the day, you can watch the real-time sky that will be visible tonight. For our overnight workers, they have a glorious sunny day to help them through their long hours. It is quite a fancy bit of technology that we have developed in conjunction with the Pacific Science Center's Planetarium. Very impressive, yes?"

"It sure is," I replied. They definitely had all the bells and whistles. It was as if we were supposed to be so impressed with the facility that we overlooked what was actually going on. We arrived at Dad's old office and knocked on the door. A skinny man with wire rim glasses answered.

"Dr. Davidoff, so sorry to bother you, but I have some very special guests with me today ..." Mr. Barron explained the situation to Davidoff and then allowed us access to his office. I scanned the stark office that was equipped with two monitors and a stack of neuroscience journals. On the floor, I found books about quantum physics and some empty peanut butter cracker wrappers.

The entire facility was only a year old, so I had never been in this office before. Dad had described it to me, but I had imagined it with plenty of furniture, plants and pictures of the family scattered about. The artificial light emitted an institutional pallor throughout the windowless, bare room. I walked around the small office, thinking about what Dad might have been working on.

Zoe had struck up a conversation with our tour guide and the nerdy Dr. Davidoff. I could tell that she was pouring it on, paying special attention to the scientist. He acted as if he rarely received that kind of attention, making it the perfect opportunity to snoop.

Walking around his desk, I looked at his open notebook. Being as inconspicuous as possible, I skimmed over his scribbling—Casimir forces ... nanotechnologies ... trouble with distance ... Alcubierre Drive, along with several formulas and notations, written haphazardly across the page. It all looked like a foreign language to me. I searched for any clue that could tell me what Dad had been working on.

I stepped backward, accidentally kicking a stack of notebooks, scattering them across the floor. Looking up, I saw that the group was engrossed in their conversation. Squatting down, I bunched the papers and notebooks back into a mound. My arms went rigid when I saw it—laying on the floor, tucked halfway into a green notebook—a single sheet of paper.

CHAPTER 27

I would recognize it anywhere, so different from my own, yet so similar. I stared at Dad's unmistakable handwriting. Glancing up, they hadn't noticed, I was in the clear. I pulled on the corner of the page and dragged it further out. There it was again—Casimir forces. A formula stretched across the page with question marks at the end. I had no idea what it meant, but I felt I was getting closer to an answer.

On the desk, the computers were on standby mode with a Biotrust logo bouncing randomly across the screen. I stood and walked to the monitors. The three others stood by the door, deep in conversation, with Dr. Davidoff leading the discussion. Reaching out, I knocked the mouse and the monitors jumped to life.

My pulse quickened and my heart leapt to my throat. A set of schematics stared at me like square eyes. There was no mistaking the detailed interior with its picket fence design — the exact drawing of my X-rayed device forged an indelible image into my mind. Dad had embedded the object displayed on the computer screen, into my Moe Berg card. Whatever Dad had been working on, Biotrust was still trying to develop. *Why would he have kept it from them? Why would it be in my card?* My mind was spinning as I joined the others, careful to keep my manner the same as when we first arrived.

"So, Van, would you care to continue the tour?" Barron asked.

"Yes, sir, I've seen everything that I need to see in here," I said. Turning to the wiry scientist, I asked, "What have you been working on recently, Dr. Davidoff?"

"Well, I have a couple of design ideas that I have come up with ..."

I bet you do, I thought as I watched him give a quick glance toward Mr. Barron.

"... but I'm not at liberty to discuss them," Dr. Davidoff finished.

"I'll fill you in on what he's shared with me," Zoe jumped in. "I think it's best that we let Dr. Davidoff get back to work."

I certainly couldn't hide anything from her. She apparently noticed a change in my demeanor right away.

"Sorry to bother you and thank you for your time," I said and walked out the door as Mr. Barron and Zoe followed me into the hallway.

"Shall we move on to the conference room where I can share more details of our operation?" Mr. Barron suggested, seeming eager to get back to surroundings that were more comfortable.

"You're the boss," I said.

We followed him to a large conference room on the main floor. Over the next hour, we listened to Mr. Barron feed us full of more propaganda than we would ever care to hear. He loaded us up with brochures and DVD's for us to use in preparing our fake presentation. After escorting us to the lobby, we quickly said our goodbyes, collected our things and bolted out the front door into the bright sunshine.

"So, what did you see in there?" Zoe asked. "I know it was something, I can read you like a book."

We followed the sidewalk to the parking garage. "I saw some incredible things that I would *LOVE* to use in our presentation," I said in an exaggerated cadence.

"*What?*" Zoe asked. Her face twisted in confusion.

"This company is conducting fascinating research to help keep America safer," I said in a ridiculous manner.

"What are you talking about?"

Arriving at the car, we jumped in and slammed the doors shut.

"Sorry, Zoe," I whispered. "There's no telling how well they can listen to our conversation while we're on their property."

We drove up to the parking attendant and I handed him the ticket.

"I hope you enjoyed your tour, Mr. Stone. Your parking fee is complimentary today. Have a nice day."

"Great, uh, thanks." I drove out, wondering how much he knew.

"Okay, now tell me what you saw," Zoe demanded as we cleared the garage.

"Our mystery device! It was on Dr. Davidoff's computer screen, without the Berg card, just the embedded device," I said.

"So, there *is* a connection."

"Did Davidoff say anything about what he was currently working on?"

"Not really, they gave me a bunch of garbage about some drugs that he's working on. His expertise is *neuro-pharmaceuticals*." Zoe gestured with air quotation marks.

"It's probably just a cover, there's no doubt that our device was on his computer."

"Your dad gave you the card just a couple of months ago, right?" Zoe asked.

"I've been thinking about that. Maybe Dr. Davidoff was assigned to the project after my dad's death to try and piece together whatever it was he was working on." I was driving aggressively and my anger was getting the best of me. "Zoe, you were right. There were two identical devices on the screen. There's another card out there."

"Let's go meet Fred," Zoe said. "I texted him to meet us at the coffee shop. Maybe his warped mind can help find a solution to this mystery."

"Don't hold your breath."

Fred sat at an outdoor table talking to a couple of women that looked old enough to be his mother. He looked up as we got out of the car and I overheard him say to his prey, "Ah, here are my younger friends, maybe we can talk again later." The two gave him a smirk that said, "Are you for real?"

With a slight lisp, Fred asked, "Guys, what took you so long?" He jumped up and moved a couple of tables over.

"Nice job, slick. Those two ladies think you're nuts," I said.

"Are you kidding me? They're *totally* into me."

"They're totally into laughing at you," Zoe said as we looked back at the two giggling women.

"What? No way, you weren't there when we discussed the current state of politics in Olympia. I had them eating out of my hands." Fred spoke like a two-year-old.

"What do you know about the current state of politics in this state?" Zoe asked, and then continued, "Anyway, what's wrong with your speech? Did you develop a lisp overnight?"

"It's my anesthesia from the dentist's office—it still hasn't worn off."

"Nice!" I said. "I'm sure your lisp helped you score major points with the ladies."

"It did! Is that genius or what?"

"You mean, you didn't you tell them you just came from the dentist?" Zoe asked.

"No way, why ruin a good thing," Fred said.

"Whatever, we have to talk about today," Zoe said.

"Yeah, let's get serious," I added then delivered an overview of the day's events. Zoe filled us in on the details of her conversation with Dr. Davidoff.

"So, now we know that Biotrust is somehow involved," said a wide-eyed Fred. "We know that Thompson was there this past weekend. Did you see any sign of the Suits?"

"Nope," Zoe and I said in unison.

"Hey, I wonder when this anesthesia is gonna wear off?" Fred picked up a fork and stabbed his chin. "This is amazing—I can hardly feel a thing."

"You're a freak," I said.

"Would you stop stabbing your face, already?" Zoe asked.

"Are you sure you're okay, Fred?" I asked.

"Yeah ... yeah, chill guys. I won't be able to enjoy it much longer."

"So, what do we do now?" Fred asked.

"I think we should talk to someone else about this," Zoe said. After a minute of silence, she continued, "How about Mr. Han? Can we get him to fill us in on that Casimir stuff?"

"Good idea, Zoe," Fred said, "but it's the middle of summer break. How do we get a hold of him?"

"Maybe we can email him. We've got his school district email," I said as I pulled out my phone. "I don't know if he checks it during the middle of summer, but it's worth a try." After a few clicks, I sent a message asking him to meet us tomorrow morning.

Zoe was lost in thought as she stared off at some clouds. Fred was in a daze. I watched as a long clear string of drool dripped from the corner of his mouth.

"Fred!" I snapped him out of his daze. "You're drooling!"

"Oh, sorry," he said, wiping his mouth. "It's a good thing my ladies aren't around!"

"Okay, let's see if Mr. Han answers back. We haven't heard anything about the card at the bank. My mom texted saying she made it to my aunt's house in Pullman. So far, we're in the clear, we just need to figure out what my dad was working on. Are we all staying at Fred's tonight?" I asked. "Did you clear it with your parents, Fred?"

"Yep, All-Star Game at 5:20, pizza at 6:00, *Rock Band* at 8:30 and sleep—never!"

"I should get home," said Zoe. "I've been gone all day and I want to grab some things to bring over tonight. I hope your parents are going to be there because my parents would kill me if they found out they weren't. My dad insisted that he drop me off at your place."

"Of course they'll be there. They can't wait to see you guys," Fred replied.

"I'll give you a ride home, Zoe," I offered.

"Don't worry about it. It's a beautiful day and the walk will do me good after being in that fortress of Biotrust."

She grabbed her stuff and walked off while fidgeting with her earbuds and iPod.

Fred and I got up and strolled to the car. "Hey, did you hear?" Fred asked. "Cantos won the Home Run Derby last night."

"No I didn't. With everything going on, I haven't seen a TV or a newspaper."

"I can't wait for him to tee off on the National League tonight," Fred said. "Man, I think this Novocain stuff's finally worn off ... too bad—I was getting some real mileage out of it."

We arrived home and I grabbed some extra clothes. I called Mom and she sounded great. We chatted for a couple of minutes. Dad's family was visiting with her all afternoon and she sounded happier than she had in a long time.

Before I left, I grabbed the backpack and its contents, and then we left for Fred's house. We drove a couple of blocks when my phone buzzed. I answered the call from Zoe.

"Van!" she shouted, her panic echoed in my ear. "I was walking ... then he came at me ... I don't know. It happened so fast ..."

CHAPTER
28

"**W**here are you?" I shouted. "Are you all right?"

"I'm fine now. I'm in my house." Her voice was rushed.

"We'll be there in two minutes. We're staying on the phone with you until we get there." I tossed the phone to Fred and floored it. Fred kept talking with Zoe, but I couldn't make out what she was saying. A rage was building inside. Someone or something had tried to hurt Zoe. I blew through a couple of stop signs with no traffic around and came screeching up to her front yard. We both jumped out and ran for the door as Zoe flung it open.

"What happened?" I asked.

"I was right over there." She had calmed down and pointed to the corner a half block over. "A car was driving slowly about a block away. Then, all of a sudden, its tires screeched, I turned and saw it coming right at me."

"Are you sure it was coming at you?" Fred asked. "Maybe it was some kids squirreling around in their car?"

"I was on the sidewalk, you moron. Cars don't normally drive toward the sidewalk. Anyway, I ran past our hedge and into our front yard before it could catch up."

Why would someone want to do this to her? After a couple of seconds, I asked, "Did you see who was driving? What kind of car was it?"

"I didn't see who it was. It looked like a generic car—dark—nothing out of the ordinary. Its windows were heavily tinted."

"Well, the good news is that you're okay. Do you still want to stay at Fred's tonight?"

"I don't want to stay here. I would rather be with you guys. I haven't even told you the worst part, yet."

My heart felt like it stopped and wouldn't beat again until it heard Zoe finish the thought.

"Right after the car took off, another car came down the street, in the opposite direction. A black sedan with—guess who?"

"The Suits?" Fred asked.

"Yep, you guessed it. They were conveniently in the area right as I was getting chased into my house."

"Thompson's people." My blood rose into my neck. I was more enraged by the second.

"Van, it's okay." Zoe must have sensed my emotion. "Nothing bad happened, I'm fine."

"Does this mean that they know the wrong card was at the bank?" Fred asked.

"I would imagine so. I figure, if they want the card bad enough, they'll find a way to contact me. Let's get inside," I said.

While Zoe grabbed her things, I said to Fred, "Why don't you take my car. I'll ride over with Zoe and her parents." I flipped him the keys and he took off.

While waiting, I sat at the kitchen table. The brightly painted room didn't help to lighten the mood. Self-doubt was creeping back in. *Was I being selfish? Was I exposing my friends to danger in order to chase a wild idea?* Zoe walked in with her backpack and sat with me.

"Do you think we should go to the police?" I asked.

"That's your call. Don't do it on my account. You have to think about your mom."

"She's hundreds of miles away and safe. I'm not sure how long that can last, though. I'm really starting to think that we might be in over our heads. The last thing I want is for you or anyone else to get hurt."

"Let's see if Mr. Han gets back to us tonight," Zoe said. "Maybe we'll learn something that will help us make a decision about what to do next. I was with you at Biotrust. If those crooks are up to something, I want to help you find out what."

"Thanks for sticking with me on this. Most people would think we're crazy," I said. Voices from the other room neared, so I ended our conversation.

"Hi, Van, are you watching the All-Star Game today?" Mrs. Harper asked.

"You bet. We're heading over to Fred's to watch the game. They have a nice fifty-five inch flat screen that makes you feel like you're right there."

"We'll see about that," Mr. Harper replied. "I want to make sure Fred's parents will be there tonight. I'm not so keen on the idea of Zoe spending the night over there, but she has been so insistent, we finally gave in."

"I'm sure it's fine," Mrs. Harper said. "Don't worry about your dad. We trust you, Zoe, and that Fred is harmless, a little goofy, but harmless. Are you guys ready to go?"

We climbed into the car and Zoe's dad talked nothing except baseball on the way over. I never realized he was such a fan.

"It must be something working with those guys. Who's your favorite so far?" Mr. Harper asked.

"It is pretty cool. Eric Cooper is great. I get him his superstition chicken every time he comes to town. Ron Cantos has been great, too," I said.

"He's one of the best. It's great to hear good things about the stars, so many of them can be such jerks."

The baseball conversation continued nonstop the rest of the ride. By the time we got to Fred's house, it sounded like her dad wanted to stay and watch the game with us.

The parents had their looking-over session, like strange dogs trying to decide if they should trust one another. Once satisfied, the Harpers left and we migrated to the TV room.

We found a giant bowl of popcorn waiting for us. The pregame introductions were on in the background, when Kathy, Fred's older sister, barged into the room.

"So, what are you little kids doing today, watching the baseball game all together? How cute!" she said.

"Just get lost and leave us alone. Why don't you go conference call your three boyfriends?" Fred shot back.

"Hey, stay out of my business."

"Why should I, everyone else is in *your business*," Fred said.

"Ugh, why did you have to be my brother? I'm so outta here."

"Good, we didn't ask you to come here in the first place."

"Hey, I smelled the popcorn. Give me a break," Kathy said.

"Just take some and get out of here, we've got work to do," Fred said.

"Ooh, work, what are you doing, trying to learn how to be more of a dork?"

"Yeah, and you're the teacher," Fred retaliated. "Get lost already."

Kathy filled a cup with popcorn and stuck her tongue out as she left the room.

"Yeah, real mature," Fred called after her. "Sorry guys, she's so lame."

"That's okay, I've seen her worse," I said.

We turned to the popcorn and dug in. Zoe asked the inevitable question, "How are we going to find out what the Berg card is all about?"

That reminded me to check my email. A reply had come in from Mr. Han, I opened it and read aloud, "Meet me tomorrow, 10:00 a.m., at the school and we can discuss."

"That's a great place to start. Depending on what we hear from him, we might know our next move," Zoe said.

"Wait, what's that?" I asked. "Fred, turn up the TV."

"… arguably the best player in baseball. We wish him the best and I know that there are over 50,000 fans here tonight that are sending their well wishes too." Joe Buck, the announcer was pouring on the schmaltz. "It's such a shame. Cantos put on quite the display last night, hitting a record forty-six home runs, eclipsing Bobby Abreu's record from 2005."

"Wow, something happened to Cantos. I wonder if he got injured last night," Fred said.

"That's amazing. I didn't know he broke the record last night. I hope it's nothing serious," I added.

We ordered pizzas for delivery. The game played in the background, but we weren't concentrating on it. Our discussion kept returning to the Berg card. Google and Bing search pages were getting a workout. We spent almost three hours researching.

A review of neuro-pharmacology led us to a dead end. There was nothing in the literature that suggested anything of national security importance. Most of the topics were about the effects of drugs on the nervous system. The common ailments in the current research included Parkinson's and Alzheimer's disease, certainly nothing that would be top secret. Depression and other psychological disorders were also big in this field. Deeper research revealed the highly profitable nature of the pharmaceutical industry. It seemed that drug companies were suing each other frequently over patents and other issues about who got there first.

Even though there was an abundance of information in the industry, I didn't feel like we were on the right track. This certainly was a big business and a lot of money was involved, but was that enough to create the kind of threats that we have been experiencing? Dr. Davidoff could be using a legitimate industry to cover what he was really working on.

"What's this *Casanova* thing you were talking about earlier?" Fred asked.

"*Casimir* forces," I answered and rolled my eyes. "I have no idea, let's check it out."

The website *Dictionary.com* reported that the Casimir effect was a net attractive force between objects in a vacuum, caused by quantum mechanical vacuum fluctuations that created radiation pressure. It went on to describe how two objects can be drawn to each other because of the lower pressure created by the wavelengths. It was important in the field of nanotechnologies. This stuff was out of my league. Even with this background information, I couldn't find a concept that would involve national security.

"Uh, guys, I'm lost. What the heck are we reading about?" Fred asked.

"I think we should ask Mr. Han about this tomorrow." Zoe yawned.

"Yeah, that's a great idea," Fred said a little too quickly and grabbed the drumsticks. "Who wants to rock out?"

CHAPTER
29

The American League won the game, which means they would get home field advantage for the World Series. Not that it mattered much for the Mariners, because they had absolutely no chance of making it that far. We played *Rock Band* until about one in the morning. I was surprised to learn that Zoe had a set of pipes on her. Fred and I crashed in sleeping bags on the couches, while Zoe slept in the guest room. Between my mind racing and Fred's snoring, it was a long night.

Fred awoke like a kid on Christmas morning and Zoe looked as if she didn't sleep a wink. I threw on a dark blue

Seahawks' hooded sweatshirt and jeans to fight against the morning chill.

"Fred, what do you think about leaving the backpack here? Would you be okay with that?" I asked.

"Don't you want to show the card to Mr. Han?"

"He's already seen it. I'd feel safer if we could leave it."

"Sure, no problem," Fred said as he tossed it into the closet.

We grabbed some bagels and ventured to the school. Although tired, my senses were on full alert. I called Mom and they were getting ready to go see the sites in Pullman. She was having a great time and it didn't sound like there was a trace of concern in her voice.

Mr. Han was waiting in the parking lot at the school with his Geiger counter in hand. "What's all the excitement about, Van?"

"We wanted to talk to you about a couple of things. What do you know about Casimir forces?"

"Casimir forces, hmmm. You are a very smart boy if you are looking into Casimir forces." He paused and looked at the other two. "Is it safe to talk around those two?"

"Of course, you know Zoe and Fred."

"Yes … yes I do. Zoe, you've always been a great student." She blushed.

"Fred, I'm still trying to figure out what's going on in that head of yours." Fred started to say something, stopped, and stood with his mouth half-open.

"Let's all go into the classroom while we uncover the secrets of quantum field theory."

We followed him through the empty hallways. He unlocked the door and grabbed a marker for the dry-erase board and we stood, forming a semicircle around him.

"Quantum mechanics or quantum field theory is considered the best way to describe the world of atoms and subatomic particles. To keep it simple, Casimir effect describes the attraction of two objects even when there doesn't appear to be an effect attracting them. The truth is, that in very small spaces, nanometers apart, two objects will be attracted because there will always be more force on the outside of the objects than between them." Mr. Han continued the explanation for another forty-five minutes, filling the board with designs and formulas.

I looked at Fred. He stared blankly at Mr. Han's diagram of the phenomenon.

"This is the problem that scientists are having in nanotechnology. As scientists reduce electrical circuits to smaller and smaller sizes, the atoms stick together and limit the speed at which microelectromechanical systems, or MEMS, work. Researchers have been questioning if you can reverse that effect and get the objects to repel each other, thereby creating a frictionless system. Once you do that, computers, cell phones, tablets and all the other electronic gadgets can get smaller and thinner."

Zoe glanced at me and I saw her *"So how does this help us?"* look. The markings of a mad scientist filled the white board. I understood what he was saying, but I couldn't figure out what that had to do with the card and holder.

A spark occurred, somewhere in the synapses of my brain, an answer formulated. "So, what you're saying is if you can repel objects by harnessing Casimir forces, then things would work faster and last longer? It would be frictionless?"

"Exactly!" Mr. Han replied.

"And if you can do that, the Casimir forces would actually cause very small objects to appear as if they are floating or levitating."

"YES!" Mr. Han was getting way too excited.

"So, if you can do that with small objects, then ultimately, you should be able do that with larger objects as well, right?"

"Ah, Van, you have always impressed me."

"I think I saw someone from MIT talking about that on one of my mom's shows. Do you think it can be done?"

"That's what scientists have been struggling with, when the object gets too big, it doesn't work. I'm sure it's only a matter of time before someone figures it out."

That someone just might have been Dad, I thought.

"Thanks for taking the time to meet with us during the middle of your summer break. You've definitely helped us understand the science a little better." Turning to my friends, I said, "Let's get going, guys."

"But ... but—won't you share with me what this is all about? You're the first students ever to ask me to come in and share my expertise. No one has ever asked me about Casimir forces before." Mr. Han's voice rose higher. "Wait— what kind of trouble are you in? Is the government after you for something? It's a cover-up, right?" Mr. Han pleaded.

"No, Mr. Han, we were just wondering about some work that Van's father might have been involved with. There are no conspiracy theories or anything like that. If we find out something conspiratorial, we'll come to you first. Thanks for meeting with us," Zoe said.

CHAPTER
30

We walked through the empty school, back to the car. After climbing in, we sat, saying nothing. I turned on the radio to break the silence. Jim Moore from *710 ESPN Radio* filled the car with chatter about the All-Star Game.

"Who's hungry?" Fred asked.

"I don't get you," Zoe griped. "We're in the middle of figuring this out and you're thinking about food?"

"Food gives us a chance to think straight," Fred said.

After a moment, I asked, "How about Ivar's, down on the waterfront? It's a beautiful day and it might help us clear our minds a little."

"That sounds good," Zoe said.

"Now you're talkin'," Fred added.

We parked the car at the house and hopped on the bus heading downtown. Parking was a real pain by the waterfront, especially in the summer.

"Hey, check this out, my mom texted a picture of her and Jake next to the cougar statue, outside Martin Stadium. Cool, it looks like everything is okay with them."

"Let me see it." Fred grabbed my phone. After a brief moment, a forlorn sigh emanated from him.

"What's wrong with you?" I asked.

"I miss Jake ..."

The salty, fishy odor of the water hit us, as we got off the bus. The loudest seagulls in the world swarmed around the docks adjacent to the original Ivar's Acres of Clams. After ordering, we sat overlooking Elliot Bay. The Fireboat, *Chief Seattle,* sat docked next to us. Behind it, a large ferry slipped out into open water, delivering tourists and commuters to the islands throughout the Puget Sound. Dive bombing seagulls screamed for handouts as we tried to talk over their noise. We lost that battle and sat eating quietly.

The fish and clam chowder, famous since 1938, hit the spot. I tossed a couple of fries to our noisy neighbors. Instantly, the number of seagulls grew exponentially as they all fought for the morsels. Zoe and Fred threw their leftovers to the birds. I watched their faces, for a moment, it was as if we didn't have a worry in the world. After we depleted our supply of scraps, we walked to the street, basking in the sunshine.

The Alaskan Way Viaduct loomed ahead of us. The concrete, double-decker, elevated roadway ran the length of downtown Seattle. Condemned, the structure had received its death sentence because of a high risk of crumbling, during an earthquake. Oblivious to that risk, thousands of cars flew over downtown Seattle every day.

We crossed the street and walked under the viaduct. The rumbling of vehicles produced a constant roar overhead, interrupted by the sporadic popping sound of cars crossing the cement joints, sounding like muffled gunshots. We turned down the road, lined with angled, parked cars on either side. The roadway above us blotted the sun, our surroundings darkened as the viaduct produced an open tunnel effect.

The old road was a mix of newer asphalt and cobblestone from a hundred years ago. Fred stumbled over the uneven roadway and almost biffed it. We walked against the flow of the one-way lane.

A car reversed out of a space and I threw my arm out to stop Zoe, who was staring toward the water.

"What a jerk, he didn't even look when he pulled out," she said.

"Give him a break. He probably didn't see us coming from this direction," I said as the tires chirped while speeding off.

"Earth calling Zoe—at least it wasn't me this time," joked Fred.

Continuing on, Zoe said, "I was a little lost in thought. Yesterday's incident sparked an investigative instinct in me. After meeting with Mr. Han this morning, I'm sure that we are on the right track. I feel like we're getting closer, but we need to figure out how to put the pieces togeth—"

She sucked in her breath, transfixed on the end of the block. Thirty yards ahead, a car rumbled. Its engine revved and four thousand pounds of metal accelerated toward us. Grabbing Zoe and Fred, I pulled them between two parked trucks as the possessed car flew by. We stood watching in disbelief as the car slammed on its brakes, fishtailed around the viaduct support and accelerated away from us.

"WHAT WAS THAT?" Fred screamed.

"Guys, we have to get out of here," Zoe shouted, "that was the car from yesterday!"

"Quick, down here." I ran to the front of the parked vehicles. We watched the crazed driver skid out of the turn.

The tinted windows looked like black holes. Moving away from us, the car sped past three support columns. Turning into a power slide, the screeching tires echoed off the viaduct. The aggressor readied for another pass.

I dropped flat in front of a parked car and watched the other two follow my lead. Breathing heavy, the smell of oily asphalt filled my nose. Pebbles and broken glass pushed into my hands and face.

My nerves sounded an internal alarm, preparing my subconscious mind for its next move. I listened to the crunching of gravel as the tires rolled by at a snail's pace. My heart raced, adrenalin flooded my body, readying it for a sprint if the sound of the rotating tires ceased. I willed it to keep moving. The seconds felt like minutes. Finally, after a short burst of burning rubber, the car disappeared up the hill into the older part of the city.

Only when the sound of the aggressor's machine dissipated, did I dare draw a breath. Moving to my knees, I peered over the hood.

"All clear. Let's get out of here." We jogged down the street and stopped against a building, checking the oncoming, one-way traffic.

Sprinting to the opposite side of the street, we moved like a one cell organism. The area under the viaduct opened up, with only one row of parked cars. Spotting an opening on the next block, I looked at my friends. They stood with wild eyes, darting in all directions.

"Let's stay together," I said. "When we make it to the next block, we'll be among lots of people. We'll be safe there. Let's go."

We hurried down the uneven one-way road, crisscrossed by forgotten railroad tracks. Out of nowhere, the attacker swung around the corner behind us, going the wrong way on the one-way street. Ahead, I spotted a chain link fence that wrapped around a raised corner parking lot.

"Go. Fence," I screamed, using the only words I could get out.

We sprinted forward as the car accelerated, gaining on us. My heart responded to the call and pounded at my chest. Zoe ran just ahead of me and I turned in time to see Fred twist his ankle on an old trolley rail. He rolled onto his back, avoiding a face-plant.

"Just run!" Fred shouted. The distance between him and the car was shrinking by the second.

Reversing direction, I took three bounding steps, reached down and grabbed his arm. "Come on. I'm not leaving you here. You can make it to the fence." We ran as if we were in a three-legged race. The car veered to the left around the last column, aiming straight for us. The deafening noise, louder than a freight train, echoed off the concrete structure.

"Aaaahhhh," I screamed, jumping onto the concrete platform. Using my momentum, I pulled Fred with me and flipped him over the fence. I leapt over as the car slammed into the concrete, just below my feet. We fell to the ground inside the chain links as concrete debris rained down on us.

The car rebounded against the wall and pulled to a stop. Scrambling, we ran for a cement column to put distance between our pursuer and us.

"Come on, hurry," Zoe called.

I pulled Fred's arm over my shoulder and we scrambled ahead. I heard the car door crunch open, metal on metal from the damaged front end. Pulling Fred with me, we dove behind the column. Through our heavy breathing, I heard a ping and felt a splatter of concrete by my ear.

"Is he *shooting* now?" Fred warbled, nearing panic.

"I would say—YES! If we stay in the shadow of this column, we can make it to the next one, and then out onto the street. There's no way he's going to follow us into a populated area."

We walked backwards, keeping the column between our attacker and us. I heard more metal crunching as the car door closed. That was our signal to run for First Avenue. Fred moved slowly, his limp was getting worse. We quickly blended with the tourist crowd as a bus approached the stop.

"There," Zoe shouted.

Frantically, I looked from side to side, and then boarded the bus and we plopped into our seats. We sat panting, trying to catch our breath.

"I guess they aren't too happy about the card you left in the bank," Fred said.

"Now, what would give you that idea?" I asked between breaths.

CHAPTER
31

The bus roared to life and carried us to temporary safety. The diesel fumes never smelled so good.

"How's the ankle?" Zoe asked.

"It's pretty sore, nothing serious. Thanks for helping me out, Van."

"What'd you think I was going to do, leave you there?"

"Call me crazy, but *yes*. It's *you* they're after, not *me*."

"You've got to be kidding. He would have run right over you."

"Okay, guys, enough," Zoe interrupted. "The important thing is that we got away. Did anyone get a good look when he stepped out of the car?" Zoe asked.

"I didn't get a good look. All I saw was the ski mask," I said disappointedly.

"That's what I saw and he was big," Zoe said.

"Okay, enough of this," Fred said in a panic. "I think we better call the cops."

My phone buzzed, I had a new text message. The number was blocked. I'd never seen that before with a text. Clicking it open, I caught my breath.

"Is your mommy having a nice trip? The games r over. Go 2 the bank by 5 and deposit berg. No cops. If u don't do as I say, someone will get hurt"

"Not so fast, Fred," I said and showed them the text.

"Van, how could they know where your mom is?" Zoe asked.

"I don't know."

"Van, we have to do it. Let's take the card to the bank, right now," Fred said, his voice shaking.

"I'm with Fred. I think we're getting into this a little too deep," Zoe added.

"You're both making perfect sense, but why do I have a strong feeling that I can't just give up the card? Something that I can't explain tells me that this won't end when I drop it off."

"So, let's go straight to the police," Fred repeated, his voice getting higher. "They'll know how to handle it."

"I lost one parent this year, I can't risk losing another." A steely confidence was growing inside as I thought about my options.

"Uh-oh, I don't like that look," Fred said.

"Don't worry, Fred. You can go home. I'll take it from here."

"Tell us what you're thinking first," Zoe said.

"Charlie, at the stadium. He's a former cop and he loves me like a grandson. Let's go talk to him. He'll know what to do."

"Do you think that's the best thing, why wouldn't we go straight to the police?" Zoe asked.

"Because if this guy knows my mom is in Pullman, then he probably has contacts—and lots of them. If he has someone in the police working for him, she won't be safe. Going through Charlie, no one will know. That'll buy us some time and we can make sure my mom is safe."

"Let's do it. Let's get off at the next stop and take the bus to the stadium," Fred said with newfound energy.

"I thought you wanted to bail?"

"I changed my mind. I can't abandon you now," Fred said as his voice returned to normal.

"Zoe?" I asked.

"Call me crazy, but I'm in."

"Fred, are you sure you're okay with your ankle?"

"I'm fine, let's go. The sooner we get to Charlie, the safer I'll feel."

Approaching the next stop, I quickly texted Mom. She responded back almost immediately, she was at a museum, and said she would call later. It seemed like she should be the least of my worries.

The bus stopped and we exited cautiously. Looking around, there was no sign of the pursuer. We crossed the street and waited for the next bus that would take us back toward the stadium. I felt like a sitting duck standing on the street. Looking at Fred, he was hardly putting any weight on his right ankle. Zoe stood, fidgeting with her hair, her normal confidence replaced with apprehension. *I shouldn't have gotten them into this*, I thought.

The bus stopped at our feet and we climbed aboard. Sitting in the back, I watched a car, parked three spaces down, pull out behind the bus. When it moved to within two car lengths, my blood turned to ice.

Without turning around, I said, "Guys, guess who's behind us." Their heads whipped around to see for themselves. I felt their collective hope escape, like air out of a balloon.

"It's the Suits," Zoe said with a surrendering sigh. Her shoulders slumped as she flopped against the seat.

"What do we do now?" Fred asked. His voice gave away his nervous, panicky state.

"Guys, we got this. Just follow me. When we get to the stadium exit, we get off and head straight into Jimmy's on First, the restaurant on the corner. It'll buy us enough time to see if they stop. Then we run across the street to the stadium and find Charlie."

The bus pulled through the light and the hydraulics let out their familiar sound. The sedan stopped at the light on the far side of the intersection. The door opened and we ran into restaurant. Looking through the window, we watched the light change. The Suits drove through the light and kept going, sitting ramrod straight in their seats, as if they didn't have a care in the world.

"Alright, let's go," I said and we ran across the street to the stadium. Charlie was at the main security gate.

"Van, how'ya doing. Have ya' been enjoying the All-Star break?" His smile stopped when he saw the serious look on my face. "What's wrong, Van?"

"Charlie, can we come in? We've got to talk to you."

"Sure, let me call Vince over here." He picked up his radio and made the call while opening the gate. Once inside the stadium, the temperature had dropped ten degrees in the shaded concourse. Charlie ushered us to a security office, unlocked the door and waved us in.

"So, what's all the trouble about, Van?"

"You remember the guys in the suits that asked you a bunch of questions last week? Well, they've been following us around. But there's more. I'm going to tell you some things that might sound crazy, are you sure you want to hear?"

"Van, you can tell me everything, there's nothin' I haven't heard before. If I find out someone's hurt you, so help me."

Starting at the beginning, I laid out everything, including the first home stand. Fred interrupted me about ten times to give his two cents. The entire time Charlie sat and listened. He only stopped us once, and said, "You can eliminate Greg from your list of suspects."

"I don't know, Charlie. What does he have in that laundry room?"

"He lost his son three years ago—Afghanistan. He hasn't been the same since. He keeps photos and letters from his son in that cabinet. I've seen 'em."

I felt a pang of guilt. Although I'd never treated him badly, maybe I didn't show him the level of compassion that I could have.

Charlie must have sensed my thoughts—he paused long enough for me to process the new information. "Tell me the rest of your story," he said.

Continuing on, I left nothing out, including that Mom was safe in Pullman. I ended with the chase that had just occurred. While I was telling him, his face was getting redder and redder.

"If anyone hurts you guys, they're going to have to deal with me. Trust me, after thirty years on the force, they don't want to be messin' with Charlie."

He paced across the room and pulled out his cell phone. "The first thing we should do is call Sergeant Waters. I broke him in as a rookie and he was my partner for ten years. I've saved his life more than once and he'll take care of you."

"Thanks, Charlie," I said, looking at the other two for confirmation. They both nodded their heads. I was finally feeling a little relieved for the first time all week.

Charlie closed his phone after a brief conversation. "There—it's done. He's waiting for you over at the police headquarters on Fifth Avenue. I told him to keep this to himself, just in case there is a stool pigeon in there somewhere. He's sending over a car with a couple of uniforms to take you to the station." He handed me a business card. "Here's my cell number. If you need anything else, you give me a call."

While we waited inside the gate, I called Mom and it went straight to voicemail. Looking up, I saw the squad car arrive. We thanked Charlie. He blushed when Zoe gave him a little hug.

"Officers Rory and Martin, we're here to pick up the suspects," a steroid laden cop said. The seams on his uniform screamed as his muscles threatened to bust out. Removing his hat, his gel-spiked buzz looked like a haircut on a three-year-old.

Charlie looked at him with a furrowed brow. "They aren't suspects. They're friends of mine and you need to get them to Waters—pronto."

"I told you these weren't criminals," the skinny Martin said as he backhanded his muscle bound partner in the chest.

"Enough of the crap," Charlie ordered. "Get them to Waters—and fast. If anything happens to them, I'm holding you two clowns responsible."

Fortunately, Fifth Avenue was only about five minutes away. We climbed into the back of the car and sat like caged animals. Martin drove and Rory turned and asked, "What'd you guys do?"

"We didn't do anything," Zoe answered.

"Well, *you are* in the back of a police car," Rory said.

"Um, we just need to see Waters about something," I said.

"Yeah, that's what they all say." He turned to Martin and said, "Hey, since we're out, I need to pick up some protein powder. Stop at the health food store on the corner."

"What? We can't do that!"

"We've been stuck on desk duty for the last month. We never get out anymore," Rory whined.

"That's because you always stop somewhere when we have a perp in the car."

"I'll only be a second. Pull over, it's right here."

Unbelievably, Martin pulled over. "You guys sit tight for a minute," Rory said, as they both got out.

"What's going on around here? What's *wrong* with these guys?" Fred whined. "I'm getting claustrophobic!"

"I'm *not* believing this," I said. The radio crackled, people passing by were looking at us like criminals. I tried the door—locked. I felt like a caged animal. I called Mom again. She was not answering her phone. I started to worry. I hoped that Waters could make a call to the police in Pullman and someone could check on her.

"There we go. Can't go a day without this stuff. We weren't too long, were we?" Rory plopped back in the passenger seat.

"Can you just get us there? We're in a hurry," Zoe said.

"Now, pretty lady, you're never in too much of a hurry for your health."

"What about my health?" Fred squealed. He was seriously losing it. "I have a broken ankle that needs immediate medical attention!"

"Hey, maybe Martin can take a look at it—he was a doctor."

"What? I was never a *doctor*!" Martin looked at Rory as if he had three heads.

"But on the way over to pick up these kids, you told me you were a doctor."

"ADOPTED. I told you I was A-DOPTED, you idiot. You better lay off the 'roids!"

"Ah—I take that back, kid. Good luck with your wrist, anyways."

I looked at the other two in disbelief. Zoe cracked a smile.

Finally, we screeched to a halt in front of the police headquarters. Laurel and Hardy led us into an empty lobby.

"I have to hit the head," Martin announced and disappeared down a hallway to the right.

"Sherry, these guys need to see—whoa." Rory spun around to assist a tall blonde female in uniform down the last couple of stairs. "My ... my Michelle, have I introduced you to my biceps, Thunder and Struck ..." His voice trailed off as he continued out of sight.

"Sorry, guys, how can I help you?" a large woman wheezed with a smile. Her uniform shirt separated between each button, revealing her industrial strength bra.

"We're here to see Sergeant Waters," I replied.

"Well, isn't he the popular guy," she said with a chuckle.

"Just a sec and I'll go get him." She moved off her seat and waddled to a door on the other end of the room. With her enormous weight, she flung the door outward and walked through. I caught a glimpse through the doorway and my body turned to steel. A uniformed officer stood talking to two men in black suits and sunglasses.

I turned to Zoe and Fred. They had seen it too. *What do we do now? The cops must be in on this too.* In an unspoken language, the three of us knew. Moving as one, we bolted out the door.

CHAPTER
32

I took the lead and ran down Cherry Street. It was all downhill. Fred fell behind with a limping gallop. The sidewalk dropped out from under me as we flew down one of the many steep sidewalks in downtown Seattle. With each step, it felt like I was floating. I grabbed a light pole and nearly swung completely around in the air as I stopped my momentum. I raced into a bagel store on the corner.

Zoe crashed through the door seconds later, followed by Fred. The three of us stood panting as a clerk looked at us like freaks.

"Can I help you?" the pimply faced clerk asked. "We're closing in a couple of minutes."

"We'll take three waters," Fred said.

Still panting, we chugged the water.

"Thanks, Fred," I said. "Now, what do we do?"

My cell phone vibrated in my pocket. I pulled it out and saw that it was Mom calling.

I punched the speaker and said, "Oh, Mom, are you okay?"

"Of course I'm okay. I'm having a great time over here. Did you know that they have a wonderful art museum?

"Uh ..." I couldn't get a word in edgewise.

"After the museum, we stopped at Ferdinands for their delicious ice cream ..."

A huge wave of relief passed through me, she sounded like a kid on summer vacation. I wanted to let her keep going, but we were in a little bit of a hurry.

"How are you getting along without me?" she asked.

"Great, I'm here with Fred and Zoe." *That didn't sound good.* "Well, I didn't mean it that way. I miss you. When do you think you'll be coming home?" I asked trying to sound as innocent as possible.

"I was thinking I'd come back on Friday, unless you want me to come home sooner?"

"NO, NO. Take your time."

"Are you sure everything is okay? You sound a little rushed."

"No, really, I'm good. I'm on my way to the stadium. I'll call you later tonight." I clicked off as she was saying goodbye.

"That's a relief, she's fine," I said.

"We've got to talk to Charlie again," Zoe said.

"What do you *mean*, he just sent us right into the last place we want to be?" Fred was losing it—again.

"I'm sure he didn't know anything about that. He would never do anything to put us in harm's way. We'll call him and tell him what happened. Maybe he can call this Waters guy and find out who the Suits are."

"Hey, you guys," the clerk interrupted. "I have to close up, so you gotta scram."

"No problem, we're out of here," Zoe offered and turned for the door.

"Wait! We have to go somewhere. We can't just go wandering outside," Fred whined. Maybe he was hurting more than I thought.

"This is Seattle, there's a coffee shop on every corner," the clerk said, shaking his head.

I looked out the window and across the street, sure enough, Seattle's Best Coffee. The light changed and the three of us hustled into the casual coffee bar.

The high-pitched, piercing sound of boiling milk blasted through the small space. The familiar smell of roasted beans comforted me for a second. At that moment, I wished that Dad were here to help us through this mess. He would know what to do next and how to get some answers out of Biotrust.

"Before I call Charlie, any other ideas?"

"Just do it," Fred said.

I punched Charlie's number into the phone and put it on speaker. They leaned in to hear over the background rumble of voices in the coffee shop.

"Van, how'd it go with Waters?"

"We didn't exactly talk to him. That's why I'm calling."

"What do you mean?"

"When we got there, the Suits were in his office. So, we took off."

"What! I'm calling that chump right now to find out what's goin' on. Where are you now?"

For a brief moment, I started to suspect that Charlie might be in on this, too. *Why would he wonder where we are?* Maybe he knew the Suits were at the precinct.

"Before I call him, you'll never guess who stopped by the stadium right after you left."

An all too familiar feeling shot through my body. This was not going to be good news.

"I don't know, who?"

"That guy who plays for the A's ... the weird one ... Thompson. I thought those guys were playing in the Midwest somewhere?"

A bolt of adrenaline hit me like a sledgehammer. *That can't be right.* "Are you sure it was him?"

"Sure as rain in Seattle. I would never forget that fella'. Something's just not right about him."

"What did he want?"

"That's the strange part. I couldn't understand why he was here. The Mariners aren't home for a week. He asked if anyone was in the visiting clubhouse. I told him no and when I asked how could I help him, he clammed up right away. He looked at me with those hollow eyes, the kind I'd seen before in my line of work. That guy is not right. Then he says to me, 'I was never here.' He turned and walked away. No cab, no car, no nothin'."

"That's it? He didn't say why he wanted into the clubhouse?"

"I'm tellin' you, Van. That was the entire conversation."

"I need to know the truth. Do you believe that Waters could be involved in whatever is going on?"

"No way. The guy is straight as an arrow. He would turn himself in for jaywalking."

"Okay, here's what I need you to do. If there is something going on, would he confide in you and be straight with you?"

"Absolutely—I've saved his life more times than I've gone to church."

Zoe and Fred had hardly breathed during the conversation. I looked around and everyone in the coffee shop went about his or her business as if we weren't even there. One guy sat with his laptop and was plugged in to his iPod, a couple of women chatted in the corner, laughing every minute or so. I was beginning to feel a little bit of relief as I continued.

"Can you call him and have him come over to the stadium—by himself—no Suits, so that we can talk through this with him and you."

"I'll call him right now and he'll drop everything to get here."

"Great, we're on our way. Thanks, Charlie. If I see the Suits or Thompson anywhere near you guys, I'm bolting."

"You got it, kid."

We hung up and Zoe said, "Are you sure we're doing the right thing?"

"It has to be, we don't have any other options. Do we?"

"My vote is with Charlie," Fred offered.

"Let's go. We'll go down to First Avenue and catch the bus back to Safeco. Let's keep our eyes open and when we hit an intersection, jump in to the first store that's open. That way we'll know if anyone is following us. It might take us a little while, but I'd rather be safe."

"I gotta take a leak before we go," Fred said while dancing on his injured ankle. We all realized that he was right and made a pit stop before leaving.

CHAPTER
33

Feeling a bit relieved, we huddled by the entrance and looked in both directions. Bolting out the door, Zoe and Fred fell in step as we mixed with the pedestrians crossing at the light. A block later, surrounded by empty parking lots, I felt a moment of panic. My heart increased its cadence, while I looked for the protection of the buildings. A right turn took us north—I looked back and saw the same look of concern on Zoe and Fred. All of the streets leading North-South were out in the open with no place to hide. As I turned west on Columbia, I picked up my pace and was momentarily

blinded by the lowering sun, reflecting off of Puget Sound—
its brilliance magnified by the tall, glass buildings.

Cars now packed the street. There was no way anyone
could follow us, except on foot. The downhill momentum
carried us faster as we reached Third Avenue. I hurried into
a drugstore on the corner and within seconds, our group
reformed.

"Only two more blocks and we're home free," I said.

"I was getting pretty freaked out, up there," Fred said.
"There wasn't any place to hide. We were easy pickings!"
Fred looked frazzled. Zoe didn't say a word, but I could tell
her mind was going a mile-a-minute.

A huge crowd disembarked from the bus stop on Third.
"Here's our chance, just mix in with the crowd. Let's go," I
said.

We made a break for it and disappeared into the crowd.
Crossing the street, I hurriedly walked under a row of trees
growing right out of the sidewalk. The big, leafy branches
soared over our heads, nature's way of providing protection
to those below, for us, it was a false security.

We weaved our way through commuters waiting for a
bus and stopped at the light on Second—one block to go. I
stood at the corner, my foot tapping as if I had a full bladder.
Looking around, that exposed feeling crept back in.
Movement was my asylum. The light changed and we
migrated with the crowd. Not too fast, not too slow, we just
melted in with the tourists and locals. An umbrella of shade
engulfed us as we continued downhill, under the line of
trees.

Walking along a slick, marble wall, I saw First Avenue
ahead. The city had begun its transformation from modern
to century's old architecture. We stopped at the corner of
First and Columbia, scanning for a metro bus. A double-
decker, red tourist bus roared by, filled with camera toting

gawkers on the open-air deck. We crossed to the south—always moving—transitioning into Pioneer Square, amid the cobbled streets, pigeons and the homeless.

"There's a bus. Let's cross," Zoe shouted.

Our version of the ark worked its way down the narrow street. We crossed under the maples and hurried to the bus stop. I felt like it couldn't arrive fast enough, but it did so with a hiss from the brakes. As we climbed on, I saw Fred grimacing with every step.

"Fred, you've got to do something about your ankle. You can't keep running around like this," I said.

"You're right. It's really beginning to swell up. Maybe I should stay on the bus and head home."

"Do you feel safe doing that?" Zoe asked.

"Sure, whoever is after us is really after Van. They could care less about me."

"Actually," Zoe said, "they're really after the Berg card—and *that's* sitting in your closet."

CHAPTER
34

The full impact of that statement registered on Fred's face. "I have to call home. What if something happened?" He punched the speed dial. I didn't hear his conversation over the roar of the hybrid diesel-electric engine and the squeal of the brakes. I watched his shoulders relax as he hung up the phone.

"Everything's cool. But, I need to get home," Fred said.

Thankfully, nothing had happened to his family. The scope of my quandary was multiplying, putting more and more people in danger. Fred still had to go home and explain his sprained ankle. I had to end this as soon as possible.

"I know what you're thinking, Van. Don't worry—I won't say anything. I'll tell them the truth. I fell, running on the cobblestone. We'll be fine."

How did he know what I was thinking? I guess that's what friendship is really about.

We rode in silence through the Pioneer Square district. The bus moved slowly through this heavily congested area, giving me too much time to reflect. I closed my eyes for a moment. The sun blasted through the breaks in the trees at an annoying angle, projecting a strobe light pulse on my eyelids. With everything that was happening, I had forgotten that the card was in Fred's closet.

"Hey, Van ..." Fred snapped me out of my thought. I squinted at the rapid-fire of the shade and sun, like a machine gun assault on my eyes. Turning in the direction of Fred's voice, I glimpsed his ankle. "Ever since we stopped running, my ankle just keeps growing."

"That looks bad. Zoe, maybe you should go back with him."

"Van, I'm not leaving you to do this yourself. Are you crazy?"

"Fred needs to get some ice on that ankle. He needs you more than I do, right now. I've caused enough problems. I would feel better if you went with Fred, that way you can help him, he can hardly walk on that thing," I suggested, hoping that she would go with Fred. "The bus stop is three blocks from Fred's. Once you get to his house, text me to let me know you made it. You don't have to worry about me. I'm going straight to Safeco so Charlie can help us end this thing."

"I don't know," Zoe said. "I would feel better if we all stayed together. How will I know if you're okay?"

"I'll get to Charlie before you guys get back home. I'll text you, every twenty minutes. If you don't hear from me at that interval, call the police. Tell them everything. Just don't tell them that you have the Berg card. I want to hold on to it until I discover its meaning. Besides, if anything does happen to me, it's our only bargaining chip."

"Sounds like a plan to me," Fred agreed.

"I still don't like it, but we don't have many options," Zoe conceded. "Make sure that you text every twenty minutes. If you don't, it's over."

"Fair enough," I replied.

Zoe moved into the adjoining seat and hugged me. "Be careful."

I didn't respond. Part of me wanted to go back with them and pretend that this had been some type of game, a scavenger hunt. I wanted to go home and play Xbox or just hang out and enjoy the summer like any other high school kid. I knew that couldn't happen. I had to take this to its conclusion. I owed it to Dad, to find out what was in the Berg card. I owed it to Mom, to get her back home safe. I owed it to my two best friends, for sticking by me and believing in me. A determination, mixed with anxiety, grew in my gut. I was ready for whatever lay ahead.

The bus accelerated out of the old part of town as the traffic thinned. The appropriately shaped Triangle Pub flew by on the right side as the sounds of the bus echoed under a series of bridges. Qwest and Safeco fields loomed a short distance away.

I looked over at Zoe. Her eyes were watery.

"Don't do that. Everything's going to be fine, you'll see."

"I know, I know. But, I'm scared. Please, don't let anything happen to you."

The bus grounded to a stop. "Here we go. This is where I get off. Get some ice on that ankle."

I watched Zoe and Fred, looking at me from the window. Grit kicked up as the bus cleared the path in front of me. When the dust settled, reality crashed down. Across the street at the main stadium gate, an ambulance sat, blinking its warning that something bad had happened.

CHAPTER
35

My chest tightened as I watched a cop in uniform unrolling crime scene tape, while two others leaned against an unmarked car. I crossed the street and walked into Jimmy's for the second time today. Quickly, I dialed Charlie. After a few rings, his voicemail picked up and I left a message, "Charlie, it's Van. I'm across the street at Jimmy's. What's going on?"

What do I do now? I watched the scene unfold across the street. An emergency technician wheeled a stretcher through the gate and loaded it into the back of an ambulance. A siren pierced the air as they sped away.

Looking around, I saw that all eyes in the restaurant were on the commotion across the street. I walked up to the hostess. "What happened over there?"

"O-M-G ... like, I don't know! We heard this, like, popping sound, like maybe gunshots. Then people were, like, screaming. I screamed a little too."

"Gunshots? Who got shot?"

The manager walked up. "I heard that someone inside the gate was shot."

No, it can't be, I thought. *This is not right, this cannot be happening.* The manager had turned the television station from *ESPN* to the local *King 5 News.* A camera from the circling helicopter panned the area around the stadium as a voiceover explained the situation.

"We don't have much information at this time. We can report that gunshots were fired just inside the gates at Safeco Field. Fortunately, there is no event at the stadium tonight. We are getting a preliminary report that there has been an injury. The police have not released any information at this time. An eyewitness reported that he heard someone shouting. He couldn't see anything, but heard the shots. A lone gunman fled the scene, wearing a dark hooded sweatshirt and jeans. He was last seen heading east under the overpass of Royal Brougham Way. The police are searching for the assailant and have asked anyone who may have information relating to this incident, to please come forward."

The coverage returned to the studio and I looked around for answers.

"I heard that some drugged out freak lost it and just started shooting," an unknown patron said.

"Nah, that's not it, I heard someone tried to rob the ticket office," another customer offered.

The news came back on.

"This just in ... we have confirmation that there was a security officer injured in the shooting and he is being rushed to Swedish Hospital. There is no word on his condition or on the identity of the shooter. The police are still looking for the suspect who fled on foot from the scene of the crime."

No, it couldn't be. "Charlie!" I screamed. The room went silent and everyone stared at me. "I have to find out if it was Charlie." I stared at the TV monitor where a graphic displayed the description of the suspect—white male, dark hooded sweatshirt and jeans.

"Okay, kid. I'm sure they'll know soon enough."

It was the manager again. He must have seen the look of horror on my face. My mind started to tick off the events like an outline:

Thompson was just at the gate with Charlie.

I talked to Charlie.

Charlie was supposed to call his former partner to meet him.

Charlie had been shot.

I felt like all of this was my fault. *Could it be Waters?*

Looking across the street, the crowd thinned, leaving behind the crime scene team and a few cops. A film crew from *Channel 5* threw on a spotlight and started interviewing. I turned back to the live feed on the television. The graphic identified the officer as Sergeant Anthony Waters.

"... we don't have any leads. Please, let us do our job. I promise that I will find and bring this animal to justice. The victim was a former Seattle Police officer. He was my partner in my rookie days with the force. We will throw every asset toward apprehending this criminal. No more questions."

The interview ended amongst a shout of questions. It sunk in —*because of me, Charlie was injured*. He had treated me like a grandson since the first day I met him. I had to find out who did this, and everything pointed to one person. *Thompson*. However, if Thompson was with the Suits, why were the Suits in Waters' office? *Nothing is making sense*. I dialed Zoe.

"Van, we're almost to Fred's, are you with Charlie?"

"No, you're not going to believe this. Charlie's been shot."

"What?" she screamed. "How can that be?"

"I don't know, but they're taking him to the hospital. They haven't identified the shooter. He got away. Thompson was one of the last people to talk to him. What if he came back with a gun?"

"This is getting crazy," Zoe said. I could hear Fred in the background bugging her to know what was going on. "Quiet, Fred, I'm trying to listen. Where are you now?"

"I'm in Jimmy's around a bunch of people. We're watching the scene across the street and on TV. Zoe, do you think you can get to Swedish, that's where they're taking Charlie."

"Sure I can, but don't you think the police are involved now? Why don't you go across the street to the cops and tell them what's happened?"

"I can't, they described the shooter as a white male, wearing a dark hooded sweatshirt and jeans. They would consider me a suspect immediately."

"There's no way they would do that, you're a teenager in high school."

"Think about our story—it doesn't sound too convincing. We would be accusing a Major League ballplayer on a team that is traveling in the Midwest right now. How plausible is that? I've got to stay out of sight."

I heard Zoe let out a heavy sigh, and then she said, "I see what you mean. We just got to our stop. I'll call you when we get to Fred's—oh, and don't leave Jimmy's."

She hung up and I stood, staring across the street. I still didn't know what all this had to do with the Berg card and holder. *Come on, Van, think.* I watched as the cops continued to conduct their investigation across the street. Maybe Zoe was right. I should walk over to Waters and tell him everything. *Maybe Charlie didn't get a chance to call him.*

I wish Dad were here. With all of the things that were happening, it amazed me when thoughts of Dad would just appear. That empty hole in my soul just grew a little bigger. I found a chair and collapsed into it.

"Hey kid, are you all right?" the manager asked.

"Yeah, sure. I guess so." I sat there for a moment.

I rose and walked into the bathroom. Standing with arms stiffened, hands on the counter and my head hung low, my mind negotiated with the emotions. I fought the feeling of remorse, however deep inside I felt a sense of strength and conviction growing. I knew attitude was everything. It was my decision. I chose strength and conviction and put all other feelings aside. I knew that was the way that Dad would have done it. He sacrificed so that Mom and I would never have to worry for the rest of our lives. There was something big going on here and I was going to find out what—and who.

Wetting my hands, I splashed water across my face and looked into the mirror. I hardly recognized the reflection. Staring back at me was someone on a mission. A surge of adrenalin kicked in as I dried my face and hands. Shoving the door open, fearless and confident, I walked out of the room and into my future. My mind cleared—out of nowhere, a plan came together.

My phone vibrated.

"Van, we're here. Fred has ice on his ankle."

"Great, how's he doing?"

"Much better, he was walking pretty well when we got here. He's still a little whiny, but that's Fred. A couple of Advil and ice should do him wonders."

"Okay, here's what we're going to do. Let him ice for another ten minutes. Then, I want you and Fred to go to the hospital with the backpack. I'm going to catch a bus home to get my car, and then head to Biotrust. I want to find out once and for all, what Dad was working on. If I don't get answers, I'm calling the police and implicating Biotrust in the shooting at Safeco. I think I have enough evidence to do that with their connection to Thompson, and his to Charlie. You take the backpack with you. It's better if I don't have it on me when I confront Biotrust. After I'm done there, I'll check in with you for my next move."

"What do you want us to do at the hospital?"

"Go see if Debbie is working in X-ray. It's a weeknight, so most likely she is. She should be able to find out how Charlie is doing. She might know something more about what happened. If you see the Suits or Thompson, go straight to the police onsite. I'm sure the cops will be there since it's one of their own that got shot. Charlie's retired, but he's still one of them. Meanwhile, just keep tabs on the situation. If something doesn't feel right, get out of there, and then call me. Whatever you do, don't let them get the backpack."

"You got it. We'll be out of here in about fifteen. Be careful at Biotrust. I don't like the idea of you going there by yourself."

"We don't have any choice right now."

"Gotta go, I see the bus coming down First. Call me if anything changes." I clicked off and ran across the street, just as the bus pulled up. I plopped down in the front row. I felt that one way or another, this thing was coming to an end. I closed my eyes for a moment to rest. My rest didn't last long as the buzzing of my phone forced my eyes open.

I read the caller ID and I felt a wave of relief. "Hi, Mom."

"Hi, Van. I bought some of that Cougar Gold cheese that you love."

"Great, I can't wait to have some." This was getting too hard.

"Aunt Judy ran out to get some wine, so I have a little moment to myself. We've been running all day."

"You're still planning on coming home on Friday, right?"

"Yes, if that's okay with you. You sound like you miss me. Oh, I think I'm getting a little teary-eyed."

"Okay, Mom, enough with the drama. It sure sounds like you're having a great time."

"I really am, I should've done this sooner—oh, someone's at the door. I've got to get that, I'll call you right back, love you."

The call ended, my battery was almost out. *I'll have to do a quick charge at home.* The bus doors opened at the next stop and I scanned the people piling on—the usual sort of commuters, tourists and kids. I closed my eyes and almost fell asleep when my phone buzzed again.

Without looking, I answered, "Hey, Mom."

"Van Stone. Enough of your games—I WANT THE CARD," a voice bellowed.

CHAPTER
36

"I gave you another chance to drop off the card, and you didn't. I warned you, so someone had to get hurt. How does it feel to be responsible for that?" the muffled voice of the hooligan asked. "Meet me at the home plate entrance to the stadium in thirty minutes. If you don't want any of your little friends hurt, I suggest you come by yourself. Or maybe you want your mom's trip cut short?"

"You better not do anything to them." I swelled with anger.

"Then make sure you're not late—and no cops."

"How will I know who I'm meeting?"

"Oh, you'll know. You'll know exactly who I am. I WANT THE BERG CARD!"

"Don't worry, I'll be there." My anger turned to rage as I punched the phone off.

I had to call Mom and make sure she was okay. Speed dialing her number, I watched ... and waited. The screen displayed "Dialing ..." *Why is it taking so long*? The screen went blank—the battery died!

The bus pulled up to my stop. I jumped off and sprinted the two blocks to the house. The front door was ajar. I listened for a moment—silence. Standing with my back to the siding, I reached around and pushed the door open. With no sound coming from inside, I peered around the doorframe—ransacked. Confident that the house was empty, I stepped through the door. The sofa lay on its back, the buffet drawers were askew with papers strewn everywhere.

I ran upstairs and my room was the same. Scattered everywhere, my clothes littered the floor. A t-shirt draped the lamp, throwing off a strange, muted glow. Nothing was untouched, even the mattress was slightly off center.

Grabbing the landline, I dialed Mom. Straight to voicemail. *You better not hurt her*, I screamed inside my head. Running downstairs, I grabbed the keys. I raced to the car, plugged the phone into the charger and tried Mom. Straight to voicemail.

I dialed Zoe. "Where are you now?"

"We're almost to the hospital."

Talking in rapid-fire, I rattled off the situation, ending with, "... I only have twenty-five minutes left."

"No way, you're not going to meet him by yourself. That's suicide."

"I don't have any other choice now."

"But we have the Berg card."

"I know. I'm coming to meet you. Go to the hospital, see what's going on there, but make it quick. Meet me two blocks away, at O'Dea High School, in the parking lot. Bring the Berg card."

While thinking about my options, I raced up the hill to the meeting point. Every red light felt like an eternity. I had to confront the caller. That was my only chance to keep everyone safe.

I pulled into the empty parking lot. The streetlights buzzed in the darkening sky. A cloud of moths and assorted flying insects put me in a daze as I watched their dance around the lights. During the last few hours, I had felt just like the moths, bouncing around without direction—but focused on a singular mission.

Checking my phone, nineteen minutes had elapsed. I tried Mom again—straight to voicemail. I felt a growing panic. If only I could hear from Mom. A strange hate seeped from the darkest reaches of my soul. A type of blind rage that I didn't know I could possess. It sunk to my subconscious, where my true inner core converted that hate-filled rage into positive energy. The growth that I had experienced over the past few months was a result of harnessing the positive from a negative situation in my life. I was determined to conquer this using that same strength.

Headlights flashed across my eyes, immediately I recognized Fred, with Zoe driving his dad's car. I jumped out of the car. "Where's the backpack?"

"Here!" I caught it one-handed as Fred threw it over the car.

"You don't have to do this," Zoe said.

"Yes, I do, and you know that. It'll be fine—you have to trust me. I don't want anyone to get hurt."

"Hey, I sprained my ankle," Fred said.

I cracked a smile and instantly knew Fred was feeling better.

"Don't worry. I know what I'm doing." I heard myself speaking in an unfamiliar tone. "Anything to report at the hospital?"

"Yeah, the place was crawling with cops. We popped in and out, everything looked normal and there was no sign of Thompson or the Suits," Fred answered.

"We didn't have time to find Debbie," Zoe added.

"Did anyone follow you here?"

"I don't think so, we high-tailed it out through the emergency entrance, it was pretty crowded," Fred said. "Dude, who you are, you seem—different."

He noticed it, too. Ignoring the comment, I reached out and hugged Fred. "Take care, man."

Moving away, I said, "All right, I don't have much time." Zoe lunged forward and held me tight. Her eyes filled with water. *I hope I know what I'm doing,* I thought. Releasing, I jumped into the car, wondering, and not for the first time, *will I see them again?*

CHAPTER
37

Skidding out of the lot, two cars pulled out of a side street. A silver car followed me. The other, I lost in the weak beam of the streetlight. With seven minutes to get to the stadium, I rocketed down the narrow, tree-lined street. At the first chance, I fishtailed around the corner, turning right. I watched as the silver car kept to its path down the hill. I roused myself with an angry shudder, focused on my mission. While driving through the pothole-filled road, my phone rattled around in the center console, reminding me that I had five minutes to make it to the stadium.

I made a left at the next street and raced downhill. A dead end awaited me and forced me to take a one-way street, leading away from my target—four minutes until the meet time. Cursing under my breath, I worked my way west over the interstate and into the heart of downtown Seattle.

Traffic was light, but enough to slow me down. Looking like an *Erector Set*, the Seattle Public Library passed on my right. The image of my Volvo, reflected in the steel and glass structure, transmitted no hint of the stress growing inside.

Stopping at a red light on Third, I saw the pyramid top of the Smith Tower to my left. Looking down, I realized I wasn't going to make it. Two minutes remained with too many blocks to cover. Without an option, I turned left, accelerating through the red light, and raced down Third Avenue. I pushed on, ignoring traffic signals. Screeching around the corner at James, I had one minute left as I flew past a parking garage that looked like the bow of a sunken ship. "C'mon," I whispered.

I landed on First Avenue and saw Qwest and Safeco ahead. "I'm not going to make it," I told no one. Swinging left, I read the big clock on the King Street Station. I was late. Turning onto Occidental, I floored it. My phone rang— UNKNOWN NUMBER. I hit the speaker as I sprinted under the shadow of Qwest Field.

"Van, you don't follow instructions very well. You're late," my adversary said.

"I'm two blocks away."

"Too bad. I have a couple of your friends here. Would you like to say hi?"

Two voices screamed in the background.

"He got us in the parking lot after you ..."

"Van, don't give him ..."

I heard a metallic clunk—Fred and Zoe's voices instantly cut off, followed by muffled shouting.

"That's enough," he said.

I accelerated past Qwest and fishtailed around the corner at Safeco. Then it hit me, I had gone to the wrong gate. I had made an unnecessary turn. I was supposed to be on the other side, at the home plate entrance. "I'm here! Show your face ... let those guys go ... I'll give you the card."

"Van ... Van ... Van. You can't lie to me. I know you're not there yet," he said with a heavy breath. The sound thudded in my ear—I could tell he was running.

I pulled up to the home plate entrance and it was empty. This late at night there were no cars around. Sliding to a stop, I grabbed the phone and jumped out. I spun around, looking for any sign of him—nothing.

"I did my part, where are you?" I asked.

"Do you think that I would be stupid enough to actually show up there?"

"That's enough, Thompson. You don't have to hurt innocent people. I have the card—let them go."

"THOMPSON?" Hysterical laughter resounded through the phone, followed by a sharp clank. "You made me laugh so hard, I dropped my phone. Do you think Thompson is capable of this? That second-rate Minor League ballplayer? Whatever—I want you to head east along the stadium, toward the tracks. You'll see a garbage can near the outfield entrance. Wait there for me and I'll see about letting your friends out of the trunk." He hung up.

I walked slowly along the concrete. The giant green framework of the stadium drew nearer as the sidewalk sloped uphill. It wasn't Thompson. *Was it the Suits?* I was more confused now than ever.

I jumped as the ear shattering blast of a train horn rang out and reverberated off the opened retractable roof. The rendezvous point emerged about fifty yards in front of me.

Every step brought the steel girders lower on my left. My heart was about to jump out of my throat. I was defenseless.

I stopped and looked around, emptiness everywhere. I waited. The night air cooled with a sudden gust of wind. A mini whirlwind kicked up debris behind me. I spun at the noise and scanned in all directions. The seconds felt like hours as I clung to my backpack. An invisible force urged me forward as I unconsciously moved toward the garbage can.

Then I saw him. In the distance, I could make out a dark figure walking toward me, down from the overpass. He was unidentifiable with his hood pulled over his head. I stopped—my mind was racing for a solution. I felt a chill as the temperature dropped a couple of degrees.

I had to make a decision—now. My only option was to give him the card. On one condition, that he released Zoe and Fred.

My phone vibrated. "Van, don't make me do to you, what I did to Charlie. KEEP MOVING," he shouted and disconnected.

My blood boiled at the thought and my legs shifted into gear as if they had a mind of their own. The shadowy figure remained stationary. *I'm sorry Dad*, I thought. The idea of this thug getting his hands on the Berg card tore me apart. Moving slowly, twenty feet from the garbage can, my phone rang again.

"I'M MOVING," I screamed in desperation. "You can see me, can't you?"

"Van, it's me. The Suits pried open the trunk and let us out," Fred shouted. "They're on our side. THEY'RE ON OUR SIDE!"

I had a split second to decide what to do next when pure instinct took over. I jumped up to a concrete ledge that anchored the steel supports. The darkened form ran a few steps and stopped. The ping of metal on metal rang out about three feet above my head. Jumping behind an angled strut, I bought myself some time. If Zoe and Fred were safe, I wasn't going to give up.

The assailant's footsteps came faster and closer as he galloped downhill. I had to put distance between us. The steel support rose in front of me at a forty-five degree angle. I grabbed the sides and my feet found purchase on the rivets. Reaching up, I rose higher with each step as I approached a joint where six supports met. A giant attachment plate provided shelter as I muted my panting breath, straining to make myself invisible.

The dark sky, filled with cumulonimbus clouds, reflected an orange hue from the city lights. The green metal framework looked menacing amid the shadows. Looking around, a floodlight flashed into my eyes, creating temporary blind spots. Shaking my head, I determined my escape plan. Keep climbing.

My attacker reached the end of a low wall. He stopped, then resumed, slowly walking toward the spot where I had entered the structure. After looking left, then right, he lowered his hood. A gust of wind blew his dark hair. I couldn't tell who it was. He paused a moment before looking straight up.

Cantos! CANTOS? How can that be? My head started swimming as the confusion slapped me in the face. *This guy has everything. Why would he do this*?

"Van, I know you're up there somewhere. Just throw the card down and I'll let your friends go. I'll turn around and disappear forever."

The wind picked up, sending a chill through my sweat soaked body. I stood twenty feet above him—he had no clue. I didn't dare say a word. I hoped that Fred and Zoe would bring help before he had a chance to make a move.

"Come on, Van. Do what's best for you. You probably thought we were buddies, didn't you. Fat chance, you were ripe for the taking. I remember how clueless you were those first few days."

My anger grew with each second. I had so many questions, but didn't dare speak. He walked uphill and with a hop, he pulled himself onto the concrete base.

"We can make this real simple. I have your friends in the trunk. Throw me the card and I'll let your friends out. What don't you understand about that? I don't even know what's so important about the stupid card. I just know that some people want it enough to kill for it. Whatever—it's your lame dad's fault, anyway. He had to go and hide something in that card. Why would he want to put his own son in danger? Sounds like my dad, you think you know someone … and bam, they turn out completely different."

No—Dad would never have done anything to hurt me, I thought. Shaking off his words, I held the backpack tighter. I looked up at my next move and realized that the beam climbed at a much steeper angle, about sixty degrees and twice has high.

"This was not the way it was supposed to go down. Sorry, *buddy*," he said with sarcasm.

He didn't know where I was. I watched as he shimmied across the concrete ledge, looking in all directions. A strong gust whipped through the framework, blowing a carabineer attached to my backpack. The high-pitched ping gave up my position as it hit the metallic beam. I was only about fifteen feet above him. His head shot up and I stared into his dark eyes. Blending in with the beam, he couldn't locate me in the shadows, but he knew I was there.

"This is not gonna end well for you," he said as he began scaling the girder. I took off, climbing like an islander up a palm tree. Each step brought me higher and farther away.

Cantos climbed directly under me, but I had a head start, putting more distance between us with every step. Aiming for the next joint, I looked down. The height was dizzying, but my adrenalin kept me focused. Grabbing the cross beam, I pulled up onto a level girder.

Two shots ricocheted in the metal superstructure. He stood at the joint where I was only moments ago. The muzzle flashed, blinding me, followed by the report of gunfire. I felt a searing pain in my left biceps. Out of reflex, my right hand reached for the pain. Losing my balance, I teetered one hundred feet above the concrete. Ignoring the pain, I wrapped my arms around an upright strut. The bullet's path burned, feeling like it was crawling with a thousand stinging ants. Looking down, my ripped sweatshirt turned dark and wet.

CHAPTER
38

The burning pain lingered, but subsided quickly as the endorphins coursing through my body took over. Fortunately, it was only a graze.

Cantos couldn't shoot if he was climbing, so I had to keep moving. Looking to my right, I saw an escalator poking through the open framework. I decided against going there—on even ground, he would overtake me in a second. To my left, a flat beam led to the back of the upper deck concourse. Like a gymnast on a balance beam, I inched my way across the metal support, one hundred feet above the ground. While concentrating on my steps, I heard Cantos getting closer.

The beams crisscrossed in the center. Stepping over the midpoint, the deafening blast of a train horn ripped through the structure, causing me to stumble. The green metal came at me with astonishing speed. I grabbed with both arms as I fell over the side, my legs dangling free.

Swinging my lower body, I latched onto the beam with my legs. My injured arm pulsed in rhythm with my heart rate. I pulled up onto the beam and lay there with my face on the cool metal.

Just ten feet away, I recognized the back of the concourse. Cantos reached the joint intersection below me and pointed the gun in my direction. I made myself as small as possible, when shots rang out again. He missed wildly as the wind picked up. I felt the temperature drop further, as the impending rain pushed the chill from the nearby water.

Unzipping my backpack, I grabbed the Berg card and stuffed it into my back pocket. "Here, take your card." I flung the backpack toward Cantos, hoping for a moment's distraction so that I could make the final ten feet. I crawled like a snake across the expanse and reached up for the fence.

"I'm not falling for that. There's no way the card is in your backpack. What do I look like?"

I hurdled over the fence onto the flat concourse. "You look like a desperate loser to me," I yelled and took off sprinting toward the retracted roof supports. The first hint of rain and small hail pelted my back as the surface grew slicker by the moment.

Looking back, I saw Cantos' hands reach for the fence. I covered the ninety feet of exposed concrete in seconds, just as Cantos leapt onto the same concourse.

In the distance, a wail of sirens drew closer. Without seeing them, I knew they were coming for me. I had to hold

Cantos off a little longer, I needed to put some distance between us. The options were few as I looked up at the crab-like structure of the retractable roof.

Another gunshot rang out and missed by a mile. *Good thing he's a ballplayer and not a sharpshooter*, I thought. I jumped over a fence, dropping eight feet to a cement slab, and rolled to a standing position. Sprinting forward, I aimed for a metal staircase that rose to the roof supports.

The wind picked up as I gained elevation. The grey water of Puget Sound, barely visible, formed an ominous background as it melded into the approaching storm. Reaching the end, I stopped on the wheel platform. I saw Cantos running below me, unaware that I had climbed higher. Looking west, the steel track extended for a few hundred feet, ending abruptly—over one hundred feet above the concrete below. With only one choice, I turned to the massive strut supporting the roof.

I gripped the cold steel of the eight-foot wheel. With only a few inches of relief, my toes clung to the surface as I sidestepped by the giant disc. Looking back, I saw Cantos standing at the fence below, searching for his prey. As I clambered to the top of the wheel structure, he spotted me. With the speed he displays in the outfield, he vaulted the fence and covered the distance to the stairs before I had even made a move.

I climbed into the strut, which formed an "A" frame over my head. Working higher, I reached the edge of the roof. The network of metal trusses formed an immense arc that gave the roof its signature look. Pulling myself up, I felt safer on the wide expanse of the corrugated metal. The rain was steady as I began my ascent through the triangular framework. If I increased my distance from my pursuer, I might hold him off until help arrived.

The rumbling of trains below muted the sounds of the sirens. I picked my way through the metal structure. Following its curve, I raised higher. The roof panels gave a little with each step. The wind and rain whipped across from my left, rendering my path even more treacherous. My shoes felt like they were made of soap. Each step required a greater effort to cover a shorter distance.

Cantos poked his head over the rooftop. "You're really stupid kid. You don't think I'm scared of heights, do you?" he yelled with a voice muffled by the wind. I didn't respond. With total concentration, I picked my way through the structure. I reached the apex of the roof's curvature and looked back. He had cut the distance between us in half. Turning away from him, I saw that the slope of the roof fell away, like a giant slide. After my first few steps, I learned that it was much harder to go down than to climb up. I carefully picked my path. To my left, the perfectly manicured baseball field lay over two hundred feet down. The "A" frame towered over my head, with its base ending at the precipice.

Simultaneously, the wind gusted and another locomotive blasted its horn. I watched as Cantos slipped and slid further away, down the sloping roof. He caught himself on a beam after sliding only ten feet. *Just fall*, I thought as I watched him recover. He stood back up, like a kid on a playground.

Slowly, I advanced down the roof, leaving myself exposed. Looking over my shoulder, I watched as he wrapped an arm around a beam and pulled out his gun. The shot ricocheted past me and I started moving faster through the framework.

The air stilled around me and I noticed an absence of sirens, leaving me with an ominous silence. A gust slammed into me from the west and the skies unleashed a torrent of frozen precipitation. The ice pellets bounced off the corrugated metal, sounding like ball bearings pouring onto a tin roof. Cantos narrowed the gap between us—less than thirty feet. The slippery metal made it impossible for me to increase my pace. He reached the downward slope and stopped.

Only twenty feet separated us. "Okay, I'll give you the card. Throw your gun down and I'll give you the card."

"My gun is my insurance policy. I'm not throwing it down. Stay right there and I'll come get it."

"NO—throw your gun down or I'll keep going. The cops will be here any second and you'll be toast anyway," I screamed over the wind and hail.

Cantos bolted from a standing position, as if stealing second base, turning it into the perfect hook slide. His sudden move caused me to jump back, losing my footing. I landed on my wounded arm and a searing pain shot through my body. The slick surface sent me accelerating down the slope. We both slid down the roof, gaining speed. Cantos gained ground as the roof's edge neared.

Continuing like this was certain death. I would plummet over the edge of the roof. I reached for a beam and grabbed, wrapping my arm tightly around its base. The inertia almost dislocated my shoulder, adding to the pain already there. Cantos instantly closed the last few feet and then slid by. I watched, and for a brief moment—I thought—actually wished—he would slip over the edge. Instead, he reached out and grabbed my ankle, nearly pulling me down with him. I kicked my leg free, changing his course—slamming him into the beam below me.

"CANTOS!"

A voice rang out from below. We both looked. Thompson was a hundred and fifty feet below, on the concourse. He kneeled with an outstretched arm, aiming a gun toward us. "It's over. Let Van go—it doesn't have to end this way."

I shook the confusion from my head. *What's Thompson doing?* With a bewildered look, Cantos stared at his teammate. Snapping out of his gaze, he started after me again. A shot rang out, ricocheting off the beam that shielded him. He reached for my leg and I yanked away.

"Come here, you little twerp," he yelled. "I'm getting tired of chasing you all over the place. GIMME THE CARD!"

With nowhere to go but up, I scrambled higher. Cantos rushed at me from behind, gaining with every step. Fatigue worked its way through my muscles. I stumbled to my knees and willed myself up again. Sweat leached into my eyes, blurring my vision. The bright green outfield filled the view on my right side, looking like a valley far below.

Suddenly, a strange noise broke through the howling wind. A helicopter lifted above the roof level, blinding me with a night-to-day spotlight. When the dots in my vision receded, I saw three ropes dangling out of the open door as the chopper neared.

Cantos took one final leap and tackled me. His gun bounced away and dropped over the edge. I fell on my back with my shoulders hanging over the edge of the roof. I watched as the gun fell two hundred feet, clanging in the outfield bleachers. He reached out and grabbed my neck.

"You've ruined my life, so now I'm going to ruin yours."

I struggled against his iron grip. It was no use. I couldn't overpower him. Spots appeared in my vision and my world turned shadowy. I felt myself sliding over the edge, unable to breathe. My lungs fought to rip every molecule of oxygen from my bloodstream. My back arched as Cantos pushed me further off the roof. My belt snagged on the lip, offering a moment of hope before the inevitable.

The shrill of the turbine engine besieged my ears, sounding oddly like a baseball card in the spokes of a bicycle wheel. The downdraft from the rotors buffeted us from a close distance as two shapes dropped from the helicopter's opening.

The noise of the chopper faded, the sound of the wind diminished, all I could hear was the thump ... thump ... thump ... of my heart pounding at my eardrums. Something knocked Cantos off me and the force on my trachea released. I sucked in—air rushed back into my lungs. Life sustaining oxygen flooded back into my body, my eyes cleared in time to realize—it was too late.

I felt weightless. Panicking, I realized—I was weightless. My legs slid across the lip, as my head pointed to the seats below. Frantically, I clamped my feet onto the roof's edge. My arms flailed, grabbing at the air, but my momentum was too much. My feet could not hold. I dropped.

CHAPTER
39

In that fraction of a second, I wondered if Mom was safe, if Fred's ankle was better, was Charlie okay and I realized, I hadn't said goodbye to Zoe. A strange wind battered me, as I read an upside-down "Welcome to Safeco Field" sign. A blur flashed on my right side. Instantly, my upper body stopped. Inertia generated a centrifugal force, whipping my legs underneath. The world returned to its normal position. I dangled from the arm of a SWAT member, suspended by rope from the helicopter cabin.

"I've got you, Van. You're okay now," he said. He reached across and wrapped a harness under my arms as we rose through the hail and the wind. Below me, the baseball diamond looked beautiful from this angle. The neat, orderly seats all faced the infield and gave it a symmetry that you would never notice from ground level. We reached the door of the helicopter and an extra pair of hands pulled me to safety.

"Where's Cantos?" I asked.

"We'll get you down first," the SWAT officer yelled over the noise of the helicopter. "He's been detained and isn't going anywhere."

I sat on the floor of the chopper as we swung away from the stadium and landed on the top floor of the adjacent parking garage. I felt safe, but I didn't have any answers. Looking out the window, I saw a small crowd. Zoe and Fred shielded the rain with their hands and looked up as we approached. Touching down about thirty feet from the gathering, the officer helped me out of the helicopter. Instinctively, we ducked down and ran out of reach of the rotors. As soon as we cleared, the aircraft leapt into the storm to retrieve the others.

Zoe rushed forward. I wrapped my arms around her and just held. The energy that binds two people started burning through my body. She held on a little tighter as if she could feel it too. Until now, the full extent of my feelings for Zoe had escaped me. Moments ago, I was two hundred feet in the air—falling, yet at this instant, I recognized that those feelings for her were profound. I realized that I had never felt this close to anyone before.

Fred hobbled up and interrupted, "Hey, what about me? Group hug!"

"Ow, watch it!" I said as Fred dug into my arm, I looked around and said, "I've got to get a hold of my mom!"

Thompson approached with the Suits on either side. "She's fine. Charlie tipped us off that she might be in danger. We sent an agent to Pullman to fly her back here."

"Agent?"

"Van, it's a long story. Let's get you out of the rain and we'll fill you in on everything."

Waters stepped in. "Looks like you took a hit on that arm. We should get you to the hospital."

"It's not bad, just grazed. Besides, I'm not going anywhere unless we're all going together." The crowd chuckled.

A SWAT van drove up the ramp, followed by a Seattle Police car. They skidded to a stop and a door flew open. Mom ran from the car. "VAN!" Jake bolted out of the open door and bounded up to me, almost knocking me over.

She grabbed me while sobbing. "Oh, Van, are you okay?" she cried. "Your arm ..."

"Don't worry, Mom, I'm alright."

"I was so scared. When they knocked on the door, I didn't know what to think. I tried calling you right away, but it kept going to your voicemail," she sobbed.

"Everything's okay now. When I got off the phone with you, my battery died. After it charged, I kept trying to reach you. I guess you were in the air by then."

The rain slackened. Staring in disbelief, I looked up at the metal arch soaring into the night sky. I had pulled off the unthinkable—and survived. I followed the light of the chopper as it returned from the structure. Officers led a handcuffed Cantos out of the helicopter. He had the look of hate on his face. We watched in silence, as they threw him in the back of a police car and drove off.

Walking arm in arm with Mom, I said, "We did it. I'm not sure what we did, but we did it. Moe Berg is in my pocket."

"Your dad would be so proud of you."

We piled into the back of the van. The Suits sat on the bench directly across from me, next to Thompson.

"What—I don't get it." I shrugged with my arms outstretched, staring at the Suits. "You guys have been following us forever. And you—Thompson—you are one of the worst ballplayers I've ever seen. What's the deal?"

Fred snorted, stifling a laugh—causing the Suits to break into a snickering bout. Waters brought his hand up to cover his mouth, his entire body convulsed as he stifled a crack-up. Unable to hold off any longer, the Suits broke into a chuckle, at the expense of their boss. Thompson hung his head low, shaking side to side. Waters couldn't contain it any longer and let out a guffaw. Smirking, Thompson raised his head and threw his arms in the air. "What?" His smirk transformed into an all out laugh. The contagious effect cascaded through the small space, and the van filled with uncontrollable laughter.

CHAPTER
40

We pulled into a parking garage on Third Avenue. A man wearing a windbreaker opened the back door of the van.

"Is this the FBI building?" Fred asked.

"Yes, Sir," Thompson replied.

"Cool."

After going through security, we rode the elevator to the twelfth floor. Following Thompson, we strode down a hallway where he opened the door to a large conference room. A smiling Len Barron, rubbing his hands, stood next to a man in a white lab coat.

"Hello, Van, my name is Dr. Stevens. Let me take a look at your arm."

"Please, help yourselves to water or coffee," Thompson said. "We brought in a variety of sandwiches. You must be pretty hungry by now."

I took off my sweatshirt. The doctor started in on my wound.

"I just want to know what's going on. Somebody needs to start talking." I winced as the doctor applied something gooey to my arm.

"Well, as you've already guessed, I'm not a great ballplayer. I am an FBI agent. I have been undercover for a while. Although, it looks like that cover may be blown. We've been following two stories for a couple of years. The first is Cantos. Two years ago, he got himself in deep with some gambling debts—nearly 1.5 million dollars. That isn't a big deal in itself. The big deal is *where* he bet his money."

Thompson walked to the head of the table and then continued. "Cantos gambled through a group that we have been watching for years. They are involved in many different crimes beyond illegal gambling. We have evidence against them for stealing corporate secrets and selling them to the highest bidder."

I took a swig of water and looked around the room. Fred was downing a sandwich and Mom watched as the doctor finished up on my arm. "But what does that have to do with the Berg card?"

"That's the other case we've been working on. You see, your dad worked on some pretty advanced projects," Thompson continued.

"You mean like levitating objects," I paused, "through the use of Casimir forces?"

Mr. Barron's eyes were wide with terror. "But ... but—how do you know about that?"

"We've been doing some research of our own, buster!" Fred said.

"Who are you?" Mr. Barron asked.

"What do you mean, who am I. I'm Van's best friend and I hurt my ankle because of your stupid device."

"Okay, everyone, let's calm down," Thompson said. "As it turns out, Van, your dad was not only a smart man, but also extremely careful. He embedded half of the mechanism for the Casimir device into your Moe Berg card. However, we did not know that. His work at Biotrust progressed until it was ready for testing. The government is very interested in this technology and Biotrust had asked us, the FBI, to keep an ear out for any chatter on the technology. This is where the two stories come together."

"We had a little security issue at Biotrust," Mr. Barron added. "We found that one of our employees in our IT department was stealing proprietary information—that's why we brought in the FBI."

"Through our counterintelligence agents, we discovered that the group Cantos was indebted to was selling the information—to foreign countries," Thompson said. His tone changed. "Biotrust research and hardware is guarded by at least three laws forbidding its sale or the transfer of its designs to foreign countries.

Mr. Barron squirmed in his chair. "This type of thing happens all the time in our industry."

"I wouldn't say that, Mr. Barron ... let's just say that you are working diligently to tighten up your ship." Thompson glared. Smiling, he turned to me and said, "I met with your dad right before the baseball season started. He provided me with the baseball card holder and a baseball card containing the other half of the Casimir levitating system. Your dad had a sense of humor—it must have been pretty tough to find a Mark Thompson baseball card."

The Suits chuckled. Thompson looked up and the chuckling immediately ceased. Continuing, he said, "Your dad explained that the holder would identify which card contained the other half of the data. He never told me that it was a Berg card, I just knew it was another baseball card."

"So, why wouldn't he have told you that I had the other card?"

"Apparently, he did not completely trust security at Biotrust or the FBI. He probably figured that it was safe with you because nobody would know—including you. Obviously, he never expected that he would not be around to put both sides together at the right time."

All heads turned to look at Fred, where a muffled sound emanated. "Show ump ..." Fred held up a finger. We all waited while he swallowed, then continued, "... so what does this have to do with Cantos? He's a Major League, All-Star ballplayer, why would he throw it all away?"

"The group to which Cantos owes the gambling debts, forced him to get the device. Through the leak at Biotrust, they found out that your dad had inserted the device into two cards. Working with the stolen plans, they were able to recreate the device that was contained in the card your dad provided to me. However, he did not leave the full plans at Biotrust when he took his leave of absence. Dr. Davidoff has been attempting to replicate the work. The component that would allow the system to function was contained in your Berg card. Eventually, they threatened to kill Cantos if he didn't recover the card," Thompson said.

"Man, we were so stupid. Cantos skipped out of the All-Star Game. We should've known that it could've been him," I said. "What I don't understand is why you wouldn't have told me about the card? You knew the holder was missing. I even remember showing you the card one day."

"That was probably an error on my part. We had a good watch on Cantos and never expected it to get out of hand. My two Assistant Special Agents, Jenkins and Taggart, that you've apparently seen quite a bit, have been tailing Cantos and watching over you."

So the Suits have names now, I thought. "That still doesn't tell me why you didn't just come forward, when you knew I had the card," I said with a little rage building.

"Cantos is just a pawn. The group he was working for is just one player in a sprawling, decentralized network. We were hoping he would lead us to the real threats, the individuals that could do some damage to national security. Once again, that was our mistake."

I looked at Mom as she started to tear up. "I want you to leave us alone. You used my son to get to your 'bad guys.' You almost got him killed," she was screaming now. "How could you do that? He would have given you the card if you had just asked."

"In hindsight, perhaps that would have been the best procedure. We are sorry that things happened as they did," Thompson said, appearing uncomfortable.

I reached over to her. "Mom, it's okay. I kept everyone out of the loop, except for Zoe and Fred. Jenkins and Taggart kept showing up and we really thought they were the bad guys. I got a note that threatened your life if I talked to anyone. We didn't know *who* was good or bad. We were ready to turn everything in to Sergeant Waters, but when we saw *those* two in there with him, we ran."

I looked around the table—no one made eye contact. "Thompson was the last one to see Charlie, so I thought Thompson shot him. After that, I knew I couldn't bring in anyone else. I didn't want anything to happen to you. The bottom line is that we're all okay. Well, except for Charlie."

"Hey, don't forget about me ..." Fred looked at me with a goofy smile.

"It's just as much our fault, Mrs. Stone," Zoe spoke up. "Van gave us an opportunity to go straight to the police, but we *believed* in what Van was doing. We knew he didn't want his dad's work to fall into the wrong hands and he was afraid for your life. "

Mom settled down and held me tighter.

"Van and Mrs. Stone, we are truly sorry about what happened to Jack," Thompson said with remorse. "He took his leave of absence on our recommendation, after we learned about the plan to steal the chip. His accident appears to be unrelated to any of these events. Our investigation revealed that it was indeed an accident. We know this has been a very tough time for the both of you."

CHAPTER
41

Looking around the silent room, I thought about everything over the past four months. Then it occurred to me. I asked, "Was my job as a batboy a set-up? What are the chances that I started working there, right under your nose?"

"No, Van, it was not a set-up. When you entered the essay contest, we did not even know you existed. Nobody knew that Jack was going to implant the device into a baseball card that he would secretly give to you. You already had the job by the time I met your dad. Contrary to the TV shows and the movies, sometimes *luck* plays a big role in solving mysteries. You earned your job all on your own and you should feel proud of that accomplishment."

My newly taped bandage crackled as I reached into my back pocket and pulled out the Moe Berg card. I sat, staring at Berg, feeling all the eyes in the room on me.

"I just received a text message from the hospital," Waters said. "Charlie is awake and doing fine. He's going to be alright."

"Can we go see him?" I asked.

"Better check with your mom."

She smiled at that. "You've been running down the 'bad guys' while I was vacationing. I think you can make your own decision."

"Let's go then, you guys want to come?"

"Of course," Zoe said.

"I'm in!" Fred said.

"We'll get you a car to take you to see him," Thompson said.

I looked around the room holding up the Berg card. "So, who gets this?"

Mr. Barron scrambled out of his chair as Thompson said, "I think we should take it for evidence." Barron froze, with his mouth hanging half-open.

"First, I need to see some identification. I can't just give it to anyone," I said with a grin.

Thompson pulled out his baseball card, while one of the assistants provided him with the holder recovered from the stadium. He positioned his card into the left side, and then handed it to me. Holding the Berg card, the magnitude of the moment was not lost. My family and friends had been threatened and injured, all because of this simple card.

I reached out, slipped the top border into the holder—and stopped. Dad's legacy was contained within this small piece of cardboard. The answers surrounding the mystery hinged on my next action.

Looking up, I saw all eyes in the room focused on the device. Len Barron rubbed his hands together and rocked back and forth, clearly agitated. Fred stared at my hand as if he was staring at a cobra—wide-eyed. Thompson sat and waited, cool as a cucumber.

The culmination of my dad's life work rested at my fingertips. At this moment, I felt a deep connection to him. I recognized that Dad had become my principal instructor in life. He instilled in me a valuable lesson.

Always believe in yourself and never give up.

I realized that I had carried that lesson with me my entire life and I could not have managed the past few hours without that fundamental concept. I felt a strange anxiety as I physically willed my fingers to liberate the card.

It broke free and settled into the holder. Nothing happened—not a sound. Then, ever so slightly, the device lifted off the table.

I stood, holding my breath. I felt as if Dad was finally at peace. Watching the phenomenon for a few seconds more, pride swelled within.

I turned to Mom and saw her cry. I knew in that instant that she had felt the same thing. Even beyond death, Dad touched and inspired those around him, filling me with a sense of awe and wonder.

The roomful of people could not take their eyes off the floating object. With unbelieving eyes, Fred lowered his head sideways, to table level—even the Suits looked at each other, astonished.

"Okay, I guess I can leave it with you," I said to Thompson. Looking at Mom, I continued, "Let's go see Charlie."

We walked to the door, with Zoe at my side. Fred limped behind, still staring at the levitation device.

I reached out for the doorknob and stopped. Looking back at Thompson, I asked, "One more thing—what's the deal with Moe Berg? Why do you think my dad chose that card?"

Thompson smiled and chuckled, "At first, I didn't know which card your dad had used. After you showed me your Berg card, an alarm went off inside. It prompted me to research the player. You see, Moe Berg played as a third string catcher for over fifteen years."

"I know that, I looked it up in *Beckett's* and the stats are on the card."

"Yes, but it was what he did during the offseason, and some speculate, *during* the season, that was of particular interest. Many believe that he worked for the Office of Strategic Services, or the OSS, the precursor to today's CIA. Later, he was a spy during World War II. Your dad was trying to send a message to you. In essence, Moe Berg … was me."

It hit me like a ton of bricks. The answer had been in front of me all along. *Man, how could I have missed that*, I thought.

"I guess I should have researched Moe Berg more and Mark Thompson less."

Fred jumped in, "Dude, is that even your real name?" A round of laughs filled the room.

"I guess you'll never know," Thompson said with a smile.

I pulled the door open and stopped when Thompson spoke again.

"Oh, and Van," He stood and picked up the device, "if you ever want a job, we could find the perfect fit for you.

"Are you kidding me? I have the best job in the world."

ABOUT THE AUTHOR

Jim Devitt spent eight years working behind the scenes in a Major League clubhouse. After his time in professional baseball, Jim graduated from Washington State University in Pullman, Washington, with a Bachelor of Science degree in Zoology, and then continued on to complete his Master of Science degree in Education from the University of Miami in Coral Gables, Florida. He has authored and co-authored numerous peer-reviewed research papers and presented at conferences throughout the country. He currently lives in Seattle, Washington with his wife Melissa and their son, Gavin.

CPSIA information can be obtained
at www.ICGtesting.com
Printed in the USA
BVHW031909180919
558802BV00001B/6/P